Dream Freedom

Dream
Freedom

SONIA LEVITIN

SilverWhistle
Harcourt, Inc.
SAN DIEGO   NEW YORK   LONDON

LEVIT

While inspired by real-life events, *Dream Freedom* is a work
of fiction and all characters in the book are products of the
author's imagination. *Dream Freedom* is meant to provide
a sense of what life is like in Sudan, a country in crisis,
torn by civil war.

Library of Congress Cataloging-in-Publication Data
Levitin, Sonia, 1934–
Dream freedom / by Sonia Levitin.—1st ed.
p. cm.
"Silver Whistle."
Includes bibliographical references.
Summary: Marcus and his classmates learn about the terrible problem
of slavery in present-day Sudan and raise money to help buy the freedom
of some of the slaves. Alternate chapters tell the stories of the slaves.
[1. Slavery—Sudan—Fiction. 2. Schools—Fiction. 3. Family life—Fiction.] I. Title.
PZ7.L58Dr 2000
[Fic] 21   00-35869
ISBN 0-15-202404-2

Text set in Stone Serif
Designed by Cathy Riggs

First edition
A C E G I J H F D B
Printed in the United States of America

12/2

For my husband, Lloyd,
with love

Contents

Foreword

This book was born from emotion. First came the shock at realizing that slavery still exists, in our own time, and that most people are oblivious to its existence. Second came the feelings of helplessness and despair. There seemed no hope of ending abuses in a land so far away and so embroiled in conflict. Rationalizing, I told myself, "There's nothing I can do about it." Then conscience and a big dose of defiance argued back, Why not? Of course something can be done. It must be done. And how else can we begin except by telling the world?

Stories are my art and my solace. They could also be my weapons. Stories give more than facts. Stories touch the conscience and stimulate action. That is my motive and my goal, to put research and study and feeling into that cauldron called the novel, to show what slavery means, not only to the captives but to all of us. For while anyone is enslaved, none of us is truly free. And in the midst of gathering tales of slavery, I discovered to my great delight a rich culture filled with beauty and dignity. I met people devoted to giving, determined to make peace and to work toward tolerance and understanding. It assured me once again that the world is filled with goodness.

Our most precious gift is freedom.

May everyone dream freedom and make that dream come true.

Acknowledgments

My sincere appreciation to and admiration for the following people, who have devoted a large portion of their lives to alleviating suffering in Sudan and elsewhere in the world. I thank them for their time speaking with me and for offering suggestions for and encouragement in the writing of this book.

Francis Mading Deng—Author, Senior Fellow,
    Brookings Institution
John Eibner—Director of Advocacy, Christian
    Solidarity International
Charles Jacobs—President, American
    Anti-Slavery Group
Jok Madut Jok—Professor, Loyola Marymount University,
    Los Angeles

Rob and Jenny Lanning—Christian Solidarity
International, U.S. Office

Theresa Perry McNeil—Christian Solidarity International,
U.S. Office

Gabriel Meyer—Filmmaker, *The Hidden Gift*

William Saunders—Executive Director, Sudan Relief &
Rescue, Inc.

Tom Tancredo—Congressman, Colorado

Barbara Vogel—Teacher

Deborah Williams—Congress on Modern Pan
African Slavery

My thanks to the Simon Wiesenthal Center, the American
Anti-Slavery Group, and Loveland Church for holding the
February 1999 symposium on slavery, which inspired this
work.

I am especially indebted to Francis Mading Deng, scholar
and statesman, for his generosity in explaining many aspects
of Dinka culture and for informing me of the current effort to
make peace in Sudan. Dr. Deng's stories and interviews with
tribal chiefs became the foundation of my own research. My
heartfelt thanks to him for his patient reading of the manu-
script and for his careful corrections on ethnographic details.

Dream Freedom

Small Things
Marcus's Story
WESTERN UNITED STATES

Marcus awakened from a wonderful dream. First he heard birdsongs, a vast difference from the sounds of cars that battled the steep grade in front of his apartment at night. At night, too, a neon sign projected its harsh flashing light onto the walls of the small living room, where Marcus slept curled against the back of the old sofa. Now he lay trying to recapture the dream. He had been riding a bicycle in the sky. He rode over and under the clouds, laughing and yelling, "Look at me! Look, I'm flying!" The bicycle disappeared, but still Marcus flew on his own wings.

The reality of morning hit Marcus with a thud. Sounds of struggle erupted all around him. His mother and Serafina were at it again.

"I don't want you hanging around with those thugs, do you hear?"

"Yes, I hear you. Everyone can hear you a mile away, Ma."

"Don't sass me, Serafina! I want you to come home from school and clean up this place. And you come alone, you hear me? This place looks like a pigpen."

"Maybe that's because pigs live here."

Marcus pulled on his clothes and hurried through the morning ritual—teeth brushed, hair combed, face washed. He was on automatic, like a machine or a robot, hurrying without thinking or feeling. Marcus wished he were invisible. Then he could slide into the kitchen, get his cereal, and take off without any hassle from Serafina or his mom. No such luck.

"Hi, Marcus." His mother looked pale. "Put those blankets away before you leave for school," she said in a monotone. Her eyes looked puffy. He could tell she was trying to sound calm. "Do you need lunch money?"

"I'll make a peanut butter and jelly sandwich," he said.

"Peanut butter's all gone," said Serafina.

"What?" exclaimed their mother.

"Paul ate it," Marcus blurted out before he had time to think.

"You creep!" Serafina screamed.

"I told you, Serafina, I don't want those boys in this house!" their mother cried.

"You little fink!"

Marcus tried to duck, but Serafina's boots, laced together, struck his arm.

"Skunk!" he shouted. "Serafina Skunk!" Tears started but he blinked them back. Grabbing a doughnut from the counter,

Marcus ran out into the hallway. The lady down the hall was locking her door. She gave him a strange look. Marcus hurried down the stairs.

"Marcus, wait!" his mom called out. "What about lunch money?"

"I've got some," he called back, his face burning with embarrassment as he nearly collided with a girl taking out trash.

Outside, Marcus stopped for a minute, gazing at the doughnut in his hand. It looked stale. Actually, he didn't feel much like eating, but he'd be hungry later, he knew. His stomach was churning, the way it always did when there were fights. The fights between his mom and Dude had sometimes lasted all night. At least Serafina had a short attention span. Short fuse, too. The thought made him chuckle, and he walked faster, remembering now that he was on the road to freedom.

Marcus felt in his shirt pocket for the baseball card, his ticket to freedom. At that very moment, four boys on bikes came riding by, yelling and laughing. One boy popped a wheelie; the others cheered. *Soon,* Marcus thought, *soon I'll be riding a bike to school, too.*

Marcus sat at the back edge of the rug, fingering the bruise on his arm. Tonight maybe she'd say she hadn't meant to hit him. You could never tell about Serafina; she was unpredictable, a little crazy. She hated it when he called her Serafina Skunk.

Miss Hazel was telling them about an article she'd read, about slaves in Sudan. "This girl is thirteen years old. Her

3

name is Akuac Malong, and she is a Dinka. She spent seven years—more than half her life—as a slave. She talks about the beatings and the near starvation and the mutilation she endured. Now she's been set free."

The girl in the photograph was smiling, showing very white teeth against black skin. Her dress was just a rag wound around her body. Miss Hazel went on, talking about the civil war in Sudan. Soldiers from the north would raid villages, stealing everything they could, burning down huts, and killing the men. Women and children were captured and taken up north as slaves. Some were as young as four or five years old.

The kids in front of Marcus were squirming. One of the girls started to cry. Marcus sucked in his breath and bit his lip. He didn't want to think about such things. Where was Sudan, anyway? Who said that article in the newspaper was true?

Suddenly he remembered the baseball card in his pocket. He took it out and held it close to his face, feeling the great comfort of knowing it was really his.

Marcus had found it at the mall just yesterday when his mom took him there for a treat and they got hot dogs for dinner. "I'm sorry we don't have much time together, Marcus," she'd said. "Things will get better. Right now I have to work longer hours, until we get back on our feet. You understand, don't you?"

They both went window-shopping, his mom on one side of the mall, he on the other. Then he saw this thing flashing like neon and he picked it up. The card was sealed in plastic, looking almost new, though the year under the picture said 1979. Marcus had felt his heart pounding as if he'd just won a 10K race.

He didn't have money to spend on baseball cards, or anything else, for that matter. He was always broke, afraid to ask his mom for money, because she'd get that tiredness in her voice. "I'm sorry, baby, I just can't do it." She'd look at the ceiling as if someone up there would help her and maybe shower down some miracles.

Now, this was a *real* miracle. Ted Williams was big time, one of the old players. The card could be worth a lot, maybe even enough for a brand-new bike. The important thing was having wheels. He could get away from the apartment, with its smell and its fights. With a ten-speed, he could ride clear up to the mountains!

Miss Hazel was still talking about the war in Sudan. "Nearly two million people have died," she said. "Can you imagine two million of *anything*?"

Marcus couldn't imagine. He had seen about twelve thousand people once in a stadium, when his mom's boyfriend, Dude, took him to a ball game. He'd had to go to the bathroom but Dude had refused to take him, so he'd just waited until he thought he'd die, because it scared him to be alone with so many strangers. What would it look like to see two million people? Miss Hazel talked about thousands more who were captured as slaves.

Marcus felt dazed. It seemed unreal, far away. Who would take people away from their homes like that? Marcus thought of how his mom walked out on Dude and brought them here to Arroyo Park to start over. It was hard to leave his old home in San Diego. He'd had buddies there. His mom had said they'd love Arroyo Park, with its mountains. They hadn't been to the mountains yet, though the snow had melted long since.

Miss Hazel held up the newspaper article. She said, "Some people are raising money to buy back slaves and return them to their homes. The price is equal to about two goats—in our money, fifty dollars. For fifty dollars this girl in the picture, Akuac Malong, thirteen years old, was set free."

Marcus looked again at the picture of the smiling girl, her dark shoulders clasped by her mother's arms. "'Her first embrace in seven years,'" Miss Hazel read.

The teacher moved to the bulletin board and pinned up the article. Just below the article hung a photograph of Mother Teresa. She looked so very old and wrinkled! She was holding a tiny brown baby in her arms. The caption said DO SMALL THINGS WITH GREAT LOVE.

Marcus wondered, *If I knew my grandmother, would she look as old and as kind as Mother Teresa?*

The recess bell rang. As Marcus rushed toward the door, Miss Hazel stopped him. "Your math homework," she said, "where is it?"

"I...I didn't do it."

"Then you'll stay after school and do it here," the teacher said. "Okay now, go on out for recess."

Marcus had planned to ask Colin about the Ted Williams card during recess. Colin was a collector and he knew everything about baseball. But Marcus didn't feel like it now. He felt kind of sick, but he didn't want to go to the nurse. She might send him home, and he didn't want to be there alone.

He glanced back at Miss Hazel. She gave him a nod and a smile. She had a look that could melt your bones, kind of concerned and tender but firm. He'd never known a teacher like Miss Hazel. He smiled back.

Words of Chiefs
DINKALAND, SOUTHERN SUDAN

BOYS, COME AND SIT here by me. Yes, come into the shade; it is pleasant and cool, and I will give you my words. Words of elders, of chiefs, are yours forever. Words given to me by my father and my father's father have made me what I am, have given me strength. Come, we will sit together. We will go later into the fields and pick the young sugarcane stalks, the sweet and new ones for your taste. Yes, when it is cool we will go and take them and fill you with sweetness. But first we will have words.

Come closer, boys, all of you. Girls, too. Well, it is a new time, and girls also must hear our words. Sit down then, and quickly, for there is much to tell. We must ponder together the nature of this catastrophe. Catastrophe is not too big a word for you, is it? It needs big words to tell the whole of it, how our people have suffered from this war.

You know, don't you, of the disaster that is our life now, the enmity and the fear. I see you on the path, in the hut, while you eat, and even in sleep looking up to the sky for the bombers that come daily. You walk with heads bowed low, looking down, hoping you will not stumble onto a mine and end like that boy over there who has but one foot. I see you. I hear your whispers. Shame, that we must speak in whispers! Shame, that our boys must look down at their feet instead of to their own uplifted spears!

The way of the world today is not as it once was when old enemies spoke together with caution, for then each knew that the other had power, though it was of a different kind. There was fear, for true, but there was also respect.

Respect is the thing that creates brothers; listen to me; it is true. Respect, not love. Love may come later—and it is a thing to cherish—but respect comes first, showing that every man has a right to sing his own melodies, to harvest, to bear, to bury his dead in his own way, to pray to God in the manner of his ancestors.

Now there are people of the north who have taken it upon themselves to decide who shall pray, and how and when. They have taken it upon themselves to decide who shall bear children and what those children shall learn. They have taken it upon themselves to judge what color of skin is good and what color is bad, and what manner of man shall be slave to which.

We must ask ourselves, you and I, in humility and beating our heads to the ground, we must ask ourselves, How have we offended God? How have we sinned, that he does not eliminate our oppressors? They say they are doing that which God desires. I say this is a falsehood. God does not desire the suffering of women and little children.

How can we bring about our redemption? How can we be set free once again?

We have tried to alter ourselves. It has not profited us. We have sent our children to the Arab schools. We have allowed our children to try on new faiths as one tries on a new garment. It has not profited us. Rather, we have become despised in their eyes and in the eyes of our ancestors. Perhaps it is the retribution of our ancestors that has cast us now into this misery. Perhaps it is the just punishment for having let go the old ways.

But hear my words, and this is true: What has happened to us is not our fate alone. My eyes have seen more changes than you can dream of in your furthest dreams. My ears have heard decrees, harsh voices, cries. A chief must have eyes and ears for everyone; how else can he rule? I know peace, and I know war. War does not belong to the victim; it consumes everyone.

Now, you know that our people are scattered. Every day brings further devastation. Famine comes to us, and we starve. Soldiers burn our fields and carry off our cattle. Other nations send food. The regime will not let it be distributed. You know, too, how food rots in the sun, while it is guarded over by militiamen with guns. You have seen the food rotting there while babies die and women want for milk, and families go at last to the camps, where they become prisoners of their own hunger—the government camps, where freedom is traded for a bowl of grain.

You young boys. Some like you are taken to be soldiers. They train you in their ways. They turn you against your own people. You young girls! They capture you and make you concubines. They fill you with children that you can never keep. Cry out, then! Cry out to God for mercy. Cry not only for yourselves but for the victor

10

and his victims. Cry for your people. I have traveled far; I have seen much. Here are the stories of our people. You must know them. When one is enslaved, none is free.

Listen, I will tell you their stories. As my ancestors are my witnesses, my words are true. Listen to the stories and learn to dream. Dream freedom.

Dabora's Song

NORTHERN SUDAN

All alone,
I dream freedom
When night surrounds me
Like a tent under a sky of stars.

Animals moan and murmur,
Cows and goats and sheep
In restless sleep;
They fold their legs and sigh.
Among them I lie uncovered,
With mist for my blanket
And hard earth my pillow,
Awake, I dream freedom.

Alone, I dream freedom;
Nobody near

To touch my hand;
No age-mates and mothers
To keep me warm,
To dry my tears;
Nobody to sing my song,
To call my name.

They have stolen my name,
Taken my birthright;
Master put a new name upon me,
Like a burden of timbers,
Like stones, pressing heavy on my back.
I do not speak that name.
I will not own that name;
It shames me.

I keep my name true,
Hear it in my heart,
Weave it into my sleep,
Grasp it like a rope
To keep me from sinking.
Name given from my mother
Name blessed by my ancestors—
With my name I dream freedom.

Daylight, I carry water on my head,
Go far to gather twigs and
Tend the beasts, bleating sheep and
Cows with udders full of milk
That I am not allowed to taste—
Warm milk that would nourish

My sinking frame.
If I drink they will beat me.

Scraps from their meal
Flung down to the dogs,
These are my sustenance,
Never sufficient. Hunger grinds
Into my bones.
My garment is ragged;
When it falls from me,
I will have none.

The smell of the goats
Lies in my hair;
My face is raw from sun and wind.
Oh, smooth butter that once my mother
Spread onto my brow
To make it shine so!
They say my skin is sinful, black;
Black is the color of a slave.

Silent, I wake to my blackness,
My bleakness,
The flies that feed on my leg
Where ropes sliced flesh
That never healed
And yellow pus drips and dries,
And pain lies upon me always
Like a net of thorns.

My legs were once strong,
My arms lithe and able,

My belly firm and teeth so white
That sisters called me beautiful;
I would bring many cows
To my family as bride-price,
And pride showed in their faces
When they saw my beauty.

I dream of beauty
Undefiled, and body whole and fine—
Mine to give willingly
In dignity and honor,
With bridewealth and feasting.
But captors roared laughter,
Mouths wide, showing teeth
And cursing, they took me.

And while I screamed,
And though I begged
And firmed my body
Like a wall,
Still they raided,
Smashed and broke,
Robbed and plundered,
And now I am not beautiful.

My mouth is stopped
Like a jug of water stuffed with rags,
Like a well in time of drought,
Like fields in famine
Bearing no grain and no greenery.
My mouth is silenced

By a knife at my throat;
I do not sing.

I dream freedom,
Without words or persons to share
The dream; if I speak
Their hands will strike,
The stick will sting,
Or ropes will bind me tight.
Mouth, be silent!
Make only silent prayer; pray freedom.

Where are my people?
I dream freedom.
I dream people with ebony faces
And gleaming eyes,
With bright teeth, lips that laugh,
Words that spill around me,
Calling, "Sister!" "Daughter!" "Beloved!"
Where are my people?

Old ones, wise with years;
Children, slim as saplings;
The young warriors,
Tall and willed with fire;
Women, bellies full of child.
Where are my people?
I lie alone and
Dream freedom.

Snake Story
Little One's Story
DINKALAND, SOUTHERN SUDAN

THEIR FACES ARE CALM. Good Dinka children, trained to endure and to be silent, they listen well without showing their hearts, even at the sorrow of Dabora's song. But the eyes tell it. Their eyes cannot conceal compassion. I will hold myself away from sorrow; they must see only my strength. The next tale is one of hope.

"Have they gone? Is it over?"

Little One calls to me. I run to peer at her inside the basket. Her small face is drawn with worry, but she does not cry. I have taught her silence. Today it is silence that saved her.

"They are gone," I say. "It is over."

I pull her out of the basket where she lay curled and hidden, that large basket I had woven with my own hands to keep dried sorghum. Into it I pushed Little One, my heart beating like war drums, for don't I know this pattern well?

17

Little One gazes out, so, with eyes very wide and round. The whites of her eyes are clear as sugar crystals, the black, darker than the deepest night. Now she looks about and she whispers, fingers tucked into her hair, "Where is the hut? Where are the goats, the cattle?"

"Come, come to me." I hold her close. I cover her eyes with my hand. If I could, I would take her away, even away from this village that I have loved since I first opened my eyes and saw sky and my own mother's face.

Dug up by hooves of swift camels and horses, clumps of ground lie uprooted now with a stench of their own. Earth, torn and broken, has its smell of dying. Ah, I know that smell.

Little One pulls away from me, stands tall. She covers her eyes against the thick, choking smoke. "Where is the hut?" she asks.

In the dusk we see forms emerging from the smoke. They shake their heads like dreamers harshly awakened; they do not want to believe what they see.

"The hut is down," I say. The word *burned* lies too hard on the tongue.

"Why did they burn it?" says Little One, angry but still without tears.

"In war," I say, "they do such things." I am thankful that until now she has not seen the full face of war, though she has lived with war from the beginning. Even I, old now, have lived with war since my youth, and yet it still seems strange that we must fear our own kind.

Little One nods slowly. "The war takes everything," she

says. "Who wanted this?" she asks, rubbing her eyes against the smoke.

"Nobody," I reply. My shoulders reach toward the sky; I feel them twisting as I search for answers. "You will ask me, Little One, the why of it. I do not know. But come, we must clear this space. Tomorrow we will begin to rebuild our hut. You and I are strong."

Little One laughs, the small tilt of a bird's call, and I must laugh, too, at the lie of an old one to a child, arms thin as twigs, shoulders narrow—the one's breasts shrunken, the other's not yet formed. We laugh at the word *strong.* Then, in our laughter, hope rises.

We begin to clear a flat round space for our *tukel,* where we will lie together at night with nothing beneath our bodies, no hides for comfort. My heart is burdened; Little One will fear the night and cry out in the dark. I tell her, "When it is dark and we lie down, I will tell you a story about an ancient event. I will tell you of when our people were at war with the snake. Snakes crept into our *tukels,* they stole food from our bowls, they lay waiting in the limbs of trees to whistle down at us, and when we were looking aside—*whish*—down they flew to tangle in our hair and spit in our faces and sometimes, sometimes they choked our breath away."

"Like the soldiers," says Little One. She looks up from the dirt where she has scraped aside a pile of pebbles and sticks so we may lie down to sleep in the place where our hut stood.

"Soldiers killed my father," she says. "He was standing in the cattle byre. My father was brave, wasn't he? And strong."

"Very brave. Very strong," I say.

"Mama they carried off," she says. It is her song, the telling of those events that she cannot possibly remember, but the heart always knows.

She knows it is I who saved her. That day, when the soldiers were gone, with the smell and the sounds of their marauding left on the ground and rising in the air, I picked up this Little One from under a mound of stones and dirt. Carefully I bathed her in warm water to ward off the chill that kills babies. I took her to another mother, to be nursed. When she was weaned, I kept her in my sight day and night. I rubbed her skin with *miok*. I bathed her eyes and combed her hair and gave her pretty bells to wear on her wrists and ankles to jingle so when she walked. Sometimes she wears skirts of flowered cloth, skirts I buy in town. Long hours I spend at the river's edge, catching fish, to dry them to sell in town so I can nurture this child.

"Come now, we will lie down." Night is coming swiftly, like a lion prowling stealthily nearby. Will we hunger all night? I had hoped to find a bit of grain remaining, to eat for our supper.

Little One reads my thoughts; she is like the wind spirit, seeing everything. "There is no grain," she tells me. "The soldiers burned it, only for spite."

I make myself busy, both hands and voice. Usually in the night the storytellers murmur until the last wakeful eye is closed. Tonight there will be no stories, for sorrow lies over the village. But I will sing, yes, I will speak stories.

"The snake, the snake thought herself better than we," I

say as Little One lies down. "Slippery and clever, crafty and strong—still, we could catch Snake in traps. We could tie her with ropes. We could kill her with fire. And we did. Often, we did."

"It was war," says Little One. She pulls up her knees, pulls in her shoulders.

We hear wailing, calling of names, long sounds like the cry of the wolf, the roar of the lion:

"O father of mine, old father, where are you?"

"Wife, woman, mother of my children—are you near?"

"No-ooo, they took my sons, both. My sons, my eyes, my life, my future."

Wailing everywhere, and smoke rising from embers that will not yet die.

Little One sits up and looks at me. "You are cold," she says.

I pull my hands down under my poor rags; they are shaking. This shaking lately does not leave me, and I fear to die, leaving Little One an orphan.

Once she had people aplenty, of course—kin on her mother's side, her mother's brothers and her father's kin, too—to care for her. The men were slain, nearly all; I heard it. I saw. Ask me not to tell you how it was done; you know. The heart knows, and the earth knows, for the earth drank in their blood. Of those remaining alive, some fled. Some were captured. The body of our village is broken; we are like a man gone lame and blind. We stumble, and we wake with amazement each morning. Somehow we few still live. But listen, I must finish the story. It is an ancient tale.

———

She trembles, Old Ma; her hands and her knees shake like young saplings in the wind. She still calls me Little One, forgetting that I grow with every rain. Soon she must see my limbs are long and firm; she will call me Amou Dabora, the name my age-mates know. Soon I will be a proper young girl, with young men coming to visit, calling out from the edge of the village, "Amou Dabora, is she here? Does she receive a visitor?"

We will talk and laugh. My friends will surround me, and we will tell jokes and riddles and laugh, oh, under the moon. Come deep nightfall, we will go into the hut specially sweetened with new grasses and flowers, and we will sit up and talk, girls and boys together, so merry! My friends will speak my virtues. His friends will tell of his strength. He will make songs to me:

> "Beloved, fly not away thus far,
>   Be here with me forever,
>   Just as the sun daily rises,
>   Just as the moon reappears,
>   Stay near forever.
>   You are beautiful as the fair-colored bird,
>   But fly not; be mine."

But what then of the marriage, the bridewealth, the singing and dancing? Old Ma told me of her wedding, how they had butchered a bull for the feast. Everyone came to eat and to dance. For me, who will dance? Who will bring plenty? Who will admire the fine cattle that the groom has brought? Our village is like an empty sack, scarcely standing. What can become of me, and of Old Ma shaking so?

She half sings, half speaks the story of the snake. "Yes, there was war between Snake and man. But one day when Deng Madut Deng was by the river, there came a snake, oh, so fierce and so strong, and before Deng Madut Deng could turn around, that snake had wound itself tightly around his chest.

"What to do? Deng Madut Deng was frightened; he saw his death before his eyes. Quickly he thought, *I must make peace with this creature.* Peace is no harder to make than war. Both need effort and skill. So he spoke to Snake in a quiet voice, 'I am going deep into the river now, and surely you will drown.'

"'Not only I will drown,' replied Snake, 'but you, also, for I know you cannot swim as long as I am on your chest.'

"Deng Madut Deng took a large step. He sank into the river up to his thighs.

"'It is my advice that you remove yourself,' he told Snake.

"'It is my advice that you stop now and let me eat you,' replied Snake.

"Deng Madut Deng took another large step. He sank into the water up to his chest.

"The snake tightened in fright. It cried out, 'I hate water! It is so cold!'

"Deng Madut Deng stood in the water until his legs became numb. At last he said, 'Let us make peace, Brother Snake. You will release me, I will step out on land, and we will both be saved. My people and snakes can be friends, why not? We will agree to live together with respect.'

"The snake spoke. 'It is well,' said he, 'but we must make a blood oath.'

" 'Bite me, then, but only to draw a drop,' said Deng Madut Deng, 'and I will bite you in turn, that our blood may mingle so we become one, like true brothers.'

"And so it was done, with respect and with fear, for each knew he could cause the other's death. In time respect turned to friendship, and so it is to this very day," says Old Ma. "My tribe has nothing to fear from snakes. My uncle was known to lie down with a snake at his head and sleep all night. In the morning Snake was still there. Uncle fed it a cup of milk and the snake left him, satisfied. So it can be," says Old Ma. "Are you asleep now?"

"Yes," I say drowsily.

"Then, good night."

I hear the shifting of Old Ma's breath, and I lie in the darkness, exploring the clouded face of the moon. Soon I hear a whisper from beyond the fire; it is Koor, the lion boy, a good friend since we were very small and not knowing about wars and such troubles.

"Come out! Come out, Amou Dabora," he calls, and I look to see that Old Ma is sleeping—shaking in her sleep.

I move slowly and silently, not to disturb her.

My friend stands waiting, his face marked with worry, thinking, *Does she yet live?*

"I am here," I call softly. "We are safe."

"I am thankful," he says, remaining distant, not looking at my face, for he is skilled in politeness, though not yet a man to come calling.

"Our hut is gone," I tell him.

"We will rebuild," says he. "Also our families, if God allows it."

I cover my mouth with my hand. "How can that be?" I say. "Families are not like seeds to spring up from the earth."

"In town," says Koor, with pride in his voice, "I have heard things, important things that are joyful, indeed, if true."

"I would be glad for some joy," I say.

"There is a trader, an Arab," says Koor.

"Arab." I spit out the word, like a bitter bud.

"Well, some Arabs are not all evil," says he. "This man performs a service. He finds captives taken to the north by the soldiers—taken as slaves."

My heart leaps terribly at the word *slaves*. It lies in my throat, thick and painful.

"This man goes and finds them," Koor says, "and buys them back." He waits, then asks, "Do you understand what I am telling you?"

"Yes. That if people are rich, they can buy back their mothers and their brothers and sisters." My tone is as bitter as the taste in my mouth.

Koor moves a few steps closer. By the rising moon I can see the whites of his eyes and his teeth and even the small moons of his fingernails.

"For the price of two goats," says Koor, "a slave can be redeemed. The son of the chief is preparing a list. He gives this list to an old woman, who gives it to the trader."

"Why does the trader do such a thing?" I ask, trembling. I wonder, *Is this trader an evil man, or is he good?*

Koor wets his lips; his forehead deepens with lines, like the lines that will be carved for him on initiation, his pride. "Well, some say he is greedy, for he lines his shoes with money and hoists it away in sacks. They say he eats meat every day of the month and drinks wine by the jug."

"A man of commerce," I say, "living on the blood of others."

Koor holds up his hand, seeing the other side as the Dinka are wont to do. "Others say he is a good man, perhaps even related to our people, taking chances to be caught and killed."

"Who would kill him?" I ask.

"The same ones who enslave us."

Koor gives me the space to think. I begin to tremble at the possibility.

"I have placed my aunts' names on the list for this trader," he finally says. "I come now to tell you what is possible, and maybe it is your wish—"

"My wish!" I cry, suddenly overcome with love and longing. "If it is possible—yes, yes, my wish to see my mother's face, to hear her voice. How can it be done?"

"Two goats," Koor repeats. "Your Old Ma sells dried fish in the village. You and she can weave baskets to sell in town. If you can save enough money to buy two goats, give the money to the trader; he will bring back your Ma. If he is able."

"Yes, yes! Put my mother's name on the list. Tell the chief yes!" I take a step toward Koor. I speak her name, the name I will never let myself forget, not even when I sleep. "Tell him, this Arab, this trader, to look for her. She is young and very beautiful, my mother, and her name is Dabora Achol Amou. I will find the money. I will bring the money. Tell him Dabora Achol Amou must be brought home, free!"

I do not sleep that night. All night I lie awake thinking of the snake story, how sometimes good can come after evil. I think of my mother's face. Might she yet come home?

The Initiation
Koor's Story
DINKALAND, SOUTHERN SUDAN

HAVE ANY OF YOU been to town, eh? Do you envy the town boys and the things they own? I have seen a timepiece on the arm; I have heard how it talks its syllables day and night. Such wonders as are in town! Listen, I will tell you of a friendship between two boys, one from town and one from the village.

All through the long rains, when the ground melted into pools of mud and both people and cattle sank in the slime, all this time I had not seen my friend Ngor Akot, age-mate and in some way cousin, for, of course, we all share bloodlines. This is the strength of our people, the purity and the pride.

But it is sad to tell it: Ngor Akot went to town and there he lived in a place like a box, with steps to go into it, and foul smells from food and heat and bodies sitting there too close, without air.

Everyone came to see him there in town. Why not? In town Ngor Akot was a worker for cash money, and with the cash money he could buy things. Aunts came to ask him for small mirrors or salve for their skin. Uncles wanted medicine for stomachaches and boils. Everybody came to Ngor Akot, and they stayed in the box room for long times, he not wishing to tell them to leave, for then it would be told everywhere that Ngor Akot was stingy and did not know his kin.

When the dry season came, I went to see him there. Oh, the smiles he showed me, and the songs he sang, happy to greet his friend and age-mate. "Is it well with you, Brother Koor? Are the cattle well, and your family? Ah, you are strong, Koor, strong as a lion and as beautiful; your mother must be proud, and your father's heart joyful for you. But come, eat something, drink."

He went to a white box, cold and shivering there on the floor, opening a light, and from it he took a bottle of orange drink. It was sweet on the tongue and cold, oh, cold as a river in the night. We sat and we drank every drop, Ngor Akot and I, exchanging our stories and our praises, as it is right for friends to do.

"You are well and strong," Ngor Akot told me, "true son of a chief. You possess the *dheeng* of your father; I see it in your walk and your ways."

I thanked my friend and praised him in return, though praise was not easy to find for one who had left the village and come to town. "You bring honor to your family," I said, "earning coin to buy cattle, to build your family's herd. All your kin respect you here. You show charity and kindness; they speak of it in the village, lo, at night, telling stories of your generosity."

I saw the rise and fall of my friend's shoulders. There he sat, hunched down, his head low. *Abid,* they call him, and he knows it, *abid,* slave of shopkeepers, drone of town dwellers, servant. But what else could he do? His father's herd, never strong, was struck by evil and many died, leaving no pride and no wealth in the family for taking brides or for barter.

"Your kinsmen send you greetings," I said, "and sing your praises every day, for you will bring them increase and honor." We nod to one another, favoring the lies. No greetings could restore Ngor's manhood. He rose, took a spear from the wall.

"Take this lucky fishing spear back with you, Koor Kuac," he said, and he clasped my shoulder. "Let it be as if part of me is with you there by the river, spearing fish."

My heart was filled with many notions as I went back home—love and fear and sorrow all leaping together, for what would become of Ngor in town? Many things befall our people in town; they are ground down like beetles, made lowly and small. All eyes in town follow the darkness of my friend, seize upon his blackness as an evil that will not fade. I sighed along the way home and thought of the grace of God, who must know the purpose of all.

Soon other thoughts crowd into my head. It is time for initiation and all the boys in my age set are throbbing with excitement and also, with dread. For to lie down and suffer deep cuts with the sharp knife, to watch the blood flow and not to run, not to scream are the true marks of a man. Will a cry be forced from my lips? Will I grimace against the seven cuts, or scream out that my head is breaking in two?

Every night as I lie sleeping, I am thinking and preparing

my *dheeng,* my courage and my manhood. How proud my mother will be! She will sing her pride to be the mother of a man who does not flinch at the blade!

As the day dawns everything is in a furor, let me tell you; the cattle seem to know! They call and cry and bellow. Oxen are decked out in bells and tassels; the women prepare butter and beer and small fried dumplings with sesame seed. Songs surround us. We boys, soon to become men, walk about, strutting, behaving much like our namesakes that the father of our group has bestowed on us, "lion men." It is the same as my given name, Koor, or Lion, and the others expect me to be a model for them. As the son of a chief I will be the first to lie down. I will be the first to rise shouting, not from pain but with joy and challenge. A man! I am a man today, fierce and strong, ready to protect, defend, defy!

Have you ever known pain? "Oh," you say, "it is a natural thing, part of life." But this pain, my brother, I tell you, is a fire without ceasing, a burning and tearing of flesh and muscle, down to bone. If a beast were to tear into a person, such would be the pain, and it does not cease. Even as the blade is held aloft, still the pain deepens and deepens until the eyes can no longer see, the lips cannot taste, the body can feel nothing but the endless torment of the flesh being sliced in two.

And into the agony comes the celebration; I was firm. I did not move or shout. My body was like a tree, firm and solid, like the horn of a bull; I did not flinch.

Pain gave way to a new elation, the certainty of my own courage. Later I would dance and leap the height of three

31

warriors, tall and tallest, filled with strength and pride. I am! I am! I am a lion man! Joy to the woman who bore me, to the mother who named me, to the ancestors who know me now as their rightful heir.

As I lay recovering, how the girls screamed and sang with joy, and the other boys watched me with envy and fear. I was the first. They would laud me. Lion man! No longer a boy.

Sometime later I, with my newly initiated age-group, set out for the cattle camp. And we were joyful that day, let me tell you, taking the cows and sheep and goats far from the village where they could feed on the sweet greenery of the season of *ker*. The light rains had fallen, and the world was a paradise of green and gold, the trees teeming with birds. How blue was the sky then, on that first day of our first cattle camp as men! On the ground all the creeping and rustling things pursue their life patterns. All are joyous at this new abundance. From the river the hippo pants as it submerges. It, too, is filled with new life and thankfulness for the rain. The crocodile, the snake, the hyena—all rejoice.

And I, newly made lion man, in my arrogance, I do not even think of my friend Ngor, who has missed it completely, until some days later when we lie about camp at night, telling stories of valor, singing songs.

There is a commotion from the edge of the camp. Someone arrives, perhaps a stranger. Everyone tenses. We have wooden clubs and shields at the ready to defend our honor and our claim. Let no other group defy us! Oh, the older set tries to intimidate us with insults shouted and sung. They will challenge us to contests; we are ready!

But it is none other than my old friend Ngor Akot, and I am astonished that he comes to show his face here in the cattle camp. Has he no pride? Or is his longing so great that he must be among us, no matter how scorned?

And scorn him they do. The initiated men turn their backs, pretending to be much occupied with their adornments and their cattle, singing songs under their breath, the theme always the same:

"Coward, coward, rejecting initiation;
See how he slinks beside us like the rat, the hyena.
Even the girls give him no glances.
He has crossed to the other way,
The non-Dinka way; let him stay apart."

I neither sing nor speak. Ngor Akot is my friend. He walks behind me, as is the way of boys regarding their elders. The others cease their taunts. This child is beneath their notice; they will not spend the breath to insult him.

My heart is heavy; we were all boys together, with our fishing spears and war spears, tending cattle, learning to be men. But now Ngor is an outsider. He tries to explain: He was detained in town. His master kept him at his tasks. We both know he could have escaped, as many do no matter what the cost, to come and be initiated, to affirm the Dinka way.

We, the newly initiated men, fill our bellies with milk and meat and butter churned for us by the admiring girls. We dance and leap and parade our favorite oxen. Mine is decorated with garlands and bells; he is dark, very dark, like me. His horns are curled, full and wide, like the thick dark hair on my head. Oh, he is beautiful, as I am handsome with my beads and ostrich feather held in my hair by a wide cloth, and wide bangles on my arm. At last we fall asleep on our beds of soft ashes.

The next day it happens. The older set comes swaggering toward us. They jeer at us. "Children, you think you are bold? Little boys, we heard you crying in the night over your cuts. Don't think you are ready to be men."

"Look at this one, he struts like a rooster. *Doodle! Doodle!* How ridiculous he looks."

"A child can outrun him. See how he twists his hip, like a girl!"

We are armed with round-ended clubs. Spears are not allowed in this fight, for the vigor of young men newly initiated is too great. We could uproot the very trees with our strength! Our actions and shouting are enough to bring down an entire village.

I have composed a song, and to my pride, others sing it now, a battle chant.

> "Power and strength to us,
>   The lion men.
>   Do not draw near, for we
>   Offer fear and pain like dagger claws,
>   Like the fierce bite of the lion.
>   Be warned!"

The girls watch and murmur behind their hands.

Pairs are quickly formed. I meet my opponent, seize my

wooden club and shield. The battle begins with circling and mumbled insults, then a shout! A leap! A blow! My club strikes his arm. He winces and darts after me. *Whack! Whack!* My shield catches the blows. We circle; we stumble; we lunge; we strike. On and on the battle goes. He is a fierce opponent, his movements swift, the blows heavy, some falling on my legs. One thrust puts me down and I lie dazed, then leap to my feet again.

Sweat streams into my eyes. My feet are on fire. A strike comes, sudden and heavy, cracking down on my shoulder. My arm buzzes from the heavy thrust, but still my hands clutch the club and the shield. I will never let go! Never!

The next blow falls on my neck. I am knocked back, my breath stopped for a moment until I swing out, hard, and now I have him. He has lost his weapon. My club touches his head. This is not a fight to the death, where skulls are cracked open. I wait, breathing heavily. An older man comes between us. "Enough," he commands. "Koor has proven his courage. You are a lion man."

I taste blood between my teeth. My left eye is swollen shut; my lips feel raw. My heart swells with pride.

Now I hear and see the other battles. The clearing is filled with noise and dust... and red-hot energy. On and on, and in the midst of it I hear sounds, the kind of sounds that blast out from a train. We have all heard and seen the train as it flashes and shrieks and roars down the tracks. And it is not imagination now, or is it? I hear the scream of the train. I feel the trembling of the tracks. I see the dust rise and feel the beating and roaring of hooves surround me. Horses! Camels! Their riders strain, rising out of their saddles, whipping the beasts, screaming, *"Allahu Akbar! Allahu Akbar!"*

What happens next is a blur of terror and confusion, so great and so deep that nobody can ever tell the same story again. It is the first time in my life I have seen real rifles. It is the first time I have ever heard the roar of a shot or seen flesh fly out and watched gut—a bleeding, slimy, stringy mass— spill onto the ground. The inside of a man, the man with whom I was caught in combat just a moment ago, the inside of him lies in the dirt. His head still moves. His eyes are glazed. And then, in that very moment, I am swept up in heat and noise and motion. I run and run and run. Around me I hear the screams of girls. I hear the bellows of cattle as they go down. I see flashing spears, but they are no match for guns. Spears break. I see round-ended clubs. One cracks loudly against a skull, a shoulder. I run and run and run.

When it is over, a haze lies over the earth, blotting the sky from the ground; all is the same, gray. The dust lies like a veil over the land, as if nature has devised a way to soften the shock. I rise to my feet. I am coated with dust and dirt and blood; my right hand hangs limp; its fingers are curled, useless.

I discover that I can walk. I walk over the places where a short time ago we strutted and sang and danced. I step on the very ground where a short time ago we met in mock battle. Now I see bodies and parts of bodies. I hear wailing: "My sister! They caught her, oh God!"

It will take more than one day to count the missing, the captured, the assaulted, the dead.

I walk to the river. No beast stirs within its watery path. The crocodile and hippo, the snakes and even the large fish have fled. The water is dark gray. Above me an owl calls. An owl by daylight is a wonder, a sign of evil and of death.

And at the river's edge, as if I have been warned afore, as if something in me knew and led me to this spot, I see my friend Ngor Akot. He lies as if he were sleeping, except that his throat is a bright stain of red, a rope of red, and into it flies are settling and burrowing, fluttering their green wings.

I take off my head cloth and lay it gently over the wound.

A Dinka man does not weep, so they say. Perhaps I am not yet a man after all. I sit and weep for my courageous friend, for my friend whose initiation now is complete.

Small Things
Marcus's Story
WESTERN UNITED STATES

"Hey, so you're a big shot now. You and your class. I saw you guys on TV."

Serafina's boyfriend, Paul, and his friend Leo were hanging around the alley with Serafina. Paul clutched the handlebars of his Yamaha, exaggerating his biceps and the blue tattoo just below his shoulder. It was a small dragon, with fierce, pointed teeth.

Marcus glanced up at Paul, then quickly averted his eyes. "We didn't do it to get on TV," he said.

"Then why did you?"

Marcus shrugged. It seemed futile to explain to Paul how they had all talked about those kids in Africa, arguing, brainstorming, at last deciding they had to do something. If it took money to get those kids free, they'd raise it somehow. Miss Hazel had gone all the way with them, getting the facts.

"It's true," she had reported back. "We could buy back some people's freedom for about fifty dollars each."

"What are we waiting for?" Krissy had called out, and everyone agreed. Once they had the project figured out, nothing else seemed as important.

After the bake sale and the car wash, after they'd raised over five hundred dollars, the kids in Miss Hazel's class were suddenly in the news. "Modern-day abolitionists," the local paper called them and wrote about "the Children's Crusade." A woman came from the local TV station, with a cameraman, to interview Miss Hazel and to photograph the class writing letters about slavery to leaders in Washington. That night, Marcus saw himself on TV—just a flashing shot, but it had felt great, just great. He'd yelled for his mom and Serafina, but by the time they came, it was over.

Paul sauntered over to Marcus, grinning. "It said you guys had a car wash and a bake sale. How sweet. What'll you do with all that dough you raised? Get it? 'Dough'?" Paul laughed and punched Leo lightly on the chest.

"We're going to redeem slaves," Marcus said, but Paul wasn't listening.

"Hey, Paul," said Serafina, "I'm tired of hanging around here. Weren't we going to go somewhere?"

"Take it easy, I'm talking to your brother. What makes you think that money ever gets to Africa? Hey, I'm talking to you, kid!"

"We sent it," Marcus said.

"How did you send it?" Paul persisted. "By airmail or pony express?"

"There's a man who takes the money and then redeems slaves." Marcus was trembling, furious. In his mind's eye, he saw that photograph of Mother Teresa and the caption DO SMALL THINGS WITH GREAT LOVE. How come Paul never heard about Mother Teresa?

"You're so dumb, Marcus. Get real. Don't you know your teacher takes the money?"

"Yeah," said Leo. "She gets you kids to be her slaves so she can take a vacation or buy herself a new car." The boys snickered.

"Come on, you guys," said Serafina. "They don't raise anything like enough for a *car*."

"Well, they just started," Paul said. He reached for Serafina, but she pulled away, stumbling over an old carton. The alley between the buildings was cluttered with trash, empty boxes, and old building materials. Paul revved up his bike. The smoke and the sound clouded around them.

"You don't know anything about it," Marcus shouted. "My teacher's been telling us all about slavery." At night sometimes, the stories burned in Marcus's mind; he couldn't shake them off. "If you knew the truth—"

"Yeah, yeah, let's go to the mall," said Leo.

"He's such a nerd," cried Paul.

"Leave him alone," Serafina said. "I mean it, Paul."

"Let's go to the mall and look at the CDs," said Leo. An old leather backpack hung loosely from his shoulder. Later it would be stuffed with things—CDs, fake jewelry, and junk food. Leo was careful. "I'm not gonna end up in jail like my old man," he always said.

Marcus felt his face flush with desperation—and with indecision. These boys were bad news. If his mother heard about this, he'd be grounded for a year, but they had transportation. And he had to get to that hobby shop at the mall to sell his baseball card.

Marcus said, "Let me go with you guys."

"What? You think I'm gonna ride you over to the mall?" said Paul. "No way. Only person I want behind me is my old lady." He beckoned to Serafina.

"Take him," said Serafina.

"He got any money?"

"I just want to go to the mall," said Marcus.

"Say *please*," said Leo. He laughed.

"Please."

"If he don't go, I don't go," said Serafina, looking tough.

"All right. Get on. Serafina, you go with Leo. Listen, kid, I don't want you grabbing me or yelling, understand?"

Marcus climbed on. He felt like a king, up high on the long, dark leather seat.

"Keep your mitts off that water bottle!" yelled Paul.

Paul took off with a roar, and Marcus hung on to his waist, excited and terrified. The baseball card was in his pocket, under his jacket. Cars zoomed past; the exhaust choked him, filling his lungs, making his eyes sting. "Yahoo!" Paul screamed out. Marcus pulled an invisible shield down over his head, focusing on the baseball card in his pocket, the money, the bike, freedom.

The Betrothal

Alier's Story
NORTHERN SUDAN

*Who shall say what is correct in such matters? Some things
are only between man and woman or between man and God. Even
a father's voice is lost when God speaks to the soul. And when a
son is returning from far away.*

When the message came from the headmaster, Alier was
startled. Had he failed in his exams? Yes, the religious studies
had been giving him trouble. Also, mathematics was difficult,
but he sat over his books far into the night, studying. He had
thought he was at the top of his form. He stood in his room,
reluctant to open the note. Usually a message meant bad
news.

Perhaps it was a matter of money. Alier had heard some of
the boys talking; tuition was going to be raised. His father

had already sold five cows to pay for his keep these last two years. Did Alier dare ask for more? There were so many things to consider. His father had to feed many mouths. His younger brothers had to be set up with their own farms, or perhaps sent to school, also—if they were fit for it, if they agreed. Alier had agreed immediately, not only because he longed to see the sights of the city but because as the oldest son, he was obligated to obey the will of his father and of the clan.

His mother's brother, Uncle Nyong, had first approached Alier on the matter of education. "You are the eldest," he had said seriously, "also the most capable. Your smile wins people, Arab and Dinka alike. You can learn the ways of the world and bring them back to us. We must be part of the modern world."

"I will go," Alier had said immediately. "But you know," he added slowly, "they will try to change me."

"They *will* change you," Uncle Nyong had said. "The question is only this: What parts of you can they change and what thoughts in your heart are unchanging forever? This is the question every man must answer for himself."

"I understand, my uncle." From that moment, Alier had felt the weight of responsibility. He felt it still, whether he was kicking a soccer ball or trying to concentrate on a difficult lesson. He was well aware that others saw him not only as himself but as he represented his entire village and tribe, even his entire people. Sometimes he heard them talking about him.

"That Dinka is smart."

"Fast on his feet."

"Yes, but you have to watch him. I'd never turn my back on a Dinka."

It was made even more difficult because of those years in the missionary school, where the Fathers had spoken to him so earnestly, so gently. "There is a path, my boy, that many before you have trod, and it leads to peace and eternal bliss. There is a house, a house of God, where the faithful will forever reside, where they will look upon his radiance and know the greatest joy imaginable."

Alier had loved the music most of all, the beautiful hymns sung by the Fathers and the choir. In the little church, he listened to their songs and gazed at the gorgeous windows and the painting of Jesus and the dozens of candles with their flickering golden glow. The beauty of it filled his heart. One night he had an unforgettable dream, a visitation. A lamb appeared, snow white, with large luminous eyes. The lamb spoke, quite like a human, its voice resonating with wisdom and love. "Back in the byre of Creation," it said, "all men were created equal, as one. All men are brothers, you see. These words were repeated by Jesus. Accept now this brotherhood. Take the name. Become a Christian."

But before Alier could choose a Christian name for himself and be baptized, it had been decided that he would leave the mission school and go to Khartoum to study in secondary school. It was a great honor. After this, if he was successful, he would go to university in Egypt, perhaps even in England. Of course, all the secondary schools were administered by Arabs. He would also have to learn the Koran. Nobody seemed to think of that except for his uncle Nyong.

"Many new ideas will fill your mind," said his uncle. "Reject those that are not right for you."

Alier had trembled inwardly. "How will I know what is right?"

"It will come to you," Uncle Nyong said. "There are always signs. They are never wrong."

The note from Alier's father lay inside its envelope, curling from the heat. Alier took it out and read it. "Your father requests that his son Alier return home for a visit to discuss a matter of family importance. It is the wish of your father that you return as soon as possible, not to neglect your obligations and studies at the school but to obtain permission from the headmaster for your departure. With greetings and all the blessings of our ancestors, your father wishes you good health and a safe journey."

It was signed by the scribe in his father's name, "Adol Wun Alier," Adol, Father of Alier. The very signature added another layer of gravity to his father's request. His father's status was tied also to him, the firstborn. If Alier succeeded, it brought honor to his father. If he failed or disobeyed the ancestors or shamed his people, his father's name was also soiled.

It took several days for arrangements to be made. The roads would be slick, as the rains had started. Also, Alier had to gain permission from each of his instructors. The math teacher, in particular, looked him up and down. The teacher's nostrils flared in distaste.

"You *abeed* always find some excuse to abandon your tasks, don't you," he had said.

Alier ducked his head. "My father requests my presence," he said. "It is out of respect for my father that I must go, but I swear to do my work just the same."

The teacher seemed amused. "An oath? An oath from a black man?" He chuckled. "Go, then. Leave your books here. They must not be soiled."

Alier nodded, backing out of the room deferentially. Outside he began to run. He had discovered that running was an acceptable way to lose his anger, and at this moment anger pounded in his head, almost overpowering his thoughts.

The run helped somewhat, but then there was the constant buzzing of questions in his head. Why had his father sent for him? Why now? Why couldn't it wait until the end of the term?

It was his father's way, he answered himself. As chief he was unaccustomed to being kept waiting.

Alier went to his friend Jima's room late the night before his departure, to say good-bye.

"Will you be back soon, Ali?" Jima asked anxiously.

"If my father allows it," Alier replied. "I hope it is not sickness that makes him send for me." Alier had not admitted his fear until now, even to himself. "My father is not old, but he has been aching in his bones for years. It is one of the reasons he has sent me to school, I think, to learn the modern medicines."

"I thought he wanted you to become a lawyer and work in the government."

"Yes. But while I am here, I do learn about other things. Pills and tonics, you know, and how to get help at the clinic. Perhaps"—Alier suddenly thought—"I will bring him back here with me. He could see a doctor."

"Would he come to Khartoum?"

"Perhaps. He is suspicious of the city. He does not like the way people look at him." Alier carefully substituted the word *people* for *Arabs,* to avoid offending his friend. "I must say good-bye now. I leave at dawn. A lorry is coming to take me all the way to the village."

"It pays to be the son of a chief," said Jima with a grin and a handclasp. "Go well, my friend. Go with Allah."

Wide-awake before dawn, Alier leaped up to prepare himself for the journey. As he was wearing khaki pants, athletic shoes, and a T-shirt, his clothes branded him instantly as a scholar, a city boy.

Alier sat back in his seat beside the Arab driver. The back of the truck was filled with produce and sacks of grain and several aging Arabs getting a ride to the next town. Twice everyone had to jump out and push, as the wheels were deeply mired and stuck fast. Alier eyed the mud on his shoes with deep regret; they were his pride. He decided he might as well take the shoes off and carry them over his shoulder. He tied the laces together, certain that the shoes on his shoulder made him look jaunty and very modern, very scholarly.

The moment the lorry came within sight of the village, dozens of small boys and girls ran out, screaming their welcome. Cows and bulls bellowed from a distance; sheep bleated. Elders rushed out of their huts, women waved and shouted, and one, his aunt, ululated loudly and long, then sang this song:

> "My nephew returns.
> He returns to us, learned and wise now,
> With city ways; welcome him!
> Praise God, give thanks and welcome!
> It is a fine day.
> We will make a feast!"

Others took up the song. The simple melody, with voices exalted as church bells, followed Alier along the dirt road. "Praise God, give thanks and welcome!"

Every step was like food to Alier's soul—the sight of the huts standing proud and firm, the dirt paths lined with stones, the cattle byres where a few goats and calves remained tethered, as it was still early and the boys had not yet gotten them out to pasture. The animals' bleating and lowing filled the air, and the songs of the cattle boys blended with the welcoming refrain.

As he approached his father's hut, Alier's eyes stung. Strange feelings pulsed through him. It felt almost as if he were returning from the dead. Everything was so familiar! Everything was so different! The knot in his throat felt like a mixture of sickness and joy.

Alier stood for a long moment in the road. The villagers now held a respectful distance and silence. Some would remember this day, the eldest son of Chief Adol returning home from Khartoum. From events like this, stories were told, songs were composed—songs of children fulfilling their duties or failing.

Outside the hut stood his father, dressed in the white garments of a chief, his head likewise wrapped, his arms decorated with many bangles. Alier had almost forgotten his father's great height, and the marks on his father's face that made him both handsome and fierce. Certainly few men ever opposed him, and his wives kept their petty quarrels to themselves, to not risk his wrath.

"Welcome, my son; you are well?"

"I am well, my father; are you well?"

"Yes. And the journey, it was good?"

"Thank you, it was fine. The women and the children, are they well?"

"Everyone is well, my son. Also the cattle thrive, except when the evil ones come raiding with their camels and horses and guns. But we do not speak of that now. Do you prosper in your studies? Do the masters speak well of you?"

"I do not yet have grades for this term, Father. I have worked hard and hope to have done well to bring honor to your name."

"That is good. Now, I see you have taken the clothing of the city, and shoes to wear for an ornament upon your chest, as we wear feathers and beads." For a moment Alier thought his father was serious; then he saw the spark of merriment in those dark eyes, and he laughed with ease and long pleasure. It was so good to laugh with one's own father!

"Come now, we speak inside together." His father led the

way. Alier ducked down and, on his knees, slipped under the low doorway, inhaling the sweet grasses that lay over the beams; the thatch on his father's hut was thick to keep out the elements. The inside of the hut was dimly lit by a small fire. Several insects buzzed around Alier's head. He kept his hands down at his sides. To swat them would imply criticism, for the smoldering coals were meant to keep the mosquitoes away.

His father reclined on the bed raised on four legs above the floor at the back of the hut. Alier took a low wooden stool and sat down, waiting for his father's words. One of the junior wives brought roasted corn on the cob. Alier and his father ate almost silently, murmuring now and then of inconsequential things.

The heat of the hut and the smell of his own body came fully to Alier now. He unbuttoned his shirt and took it off, rolled up the legs of his trousers. Among the villagers some went naked except for a cloth, and sometimes the older men preferred to discard even that. Well. It was not a matter of right or wrong but of comfort and habit, although the Fathers at the mission school had always lectured against nudity, maintaining that it led to immoral behavior.

"It pleases me that you have answered my summons so quickly, Alier." It was the signal that real talk was to begin now. "You know, of course, that the war consumes much of our energy and that we live from day to day with uncertainty."

"Yes, Father. I know this. It grieves me, too, even though I am far away in the city."

"Someday you will be a mediator for your people," said

Adol. "I know you will not remain here, perhaps only for a short time to help me and your brothers in the administration of tribal affairs."

Alier felt the sweat along his sides. He had never imagined that he might return. Others he knew about who had been educated went to distant lands, where they lived as representatives of the Dinka people or worked for large companies that extracted oil or bought gum arabic for manufacturing. You cannot go back; an eagle is not like a dog. He had soared now among educated men. He could read and write; he could argue and debate. He even knew words of English. What use was all this in the village?

His father continued, "I am not asking for much, only a commitment now, to last but a year at the longest. You owe at least that much to your people and to your ancestors. Only a year of your life."

Now Alier became aware of movement and shadows behind him as others crawled into the hut and took their places, squatting or standing along the walls. Alier was surrounded by relatives of every degree. Several women had also entered, and they kept themselves apart, their eyes downcast.

The crowd seemed to inspire Adol to oratory. In his left hand he grasped his walking staff, a symbol of authority, and he spoke with great passion, "Perhaps you do not know, because we have not wished to trouble you with these bad events, that some months ago, nearly a year ago, there was a raid upon our village. During this raid nine women and eleven little children were taken as slaves, and five old people were slaughtered here, their blood seeping into the ground."

A unanimous groan rose from the listeners. One woman began to wail loudly, "My father! My father!"

Chief Adol waited for order to be restored. Then he continued, "As you know, your cousin Magit was betrothed to a girl from a fine family—a girl he has known since childhood, namely Aluel, daughter of Yel, his firstborn child. She is a fine girl, obedient and strong; perhaps you know her, too."

"Indeed, I know her, Father," said Alier. "Several times I went with my cousin Magit to the cattle camp when he was courting Aluel. We spoke. As you say, she is a fine girl. I would be proud to have her in my family."

"Well spoken," said his father, looking pleased, and a slight sigh of relief arose from the back of the hut as the audience shifted and turned.

"Unfortunately your cousin Magit vanished in that raid. At first we thought he was murdered, as a number of our young men were caught out in the cattle camp, shot dead with bullets or dragged to the water, where their throats were slit with knives. We saw their bodies the next day, among the dust and the dung."

Adol held up his hand as the hut filled with sounds of grief and wailing. "Enough!" he said rather sharply. "I am speaking to my son, not to wring sorrow and vengeance from him but to inform him of our troubles and of his duty."

The people grew silent. Only a slight sob issued from the doorway, where the women crouched.

"Much time has elapsed," continued his father, "and we have found no body or sign of your cousin Magit, betrothed to Aluel, daughter of Yel, his firstborn."

Alier sat speechless, almost numb. The emphasis of names lent even greater urgency to what would follow.

"Now we have made many inquiries, and we must assume that he is dead."

"I am very sorry for this, my father," Alier said. He had spent many a day with his cousin Magit, for the older boy had no brothers; indeed, he was a rarity, an only child.

"We can do nothing about death," said his father. "However, there are things that we, his relatives, can and must do for the dead. If a man dies without children, there is nobody to stand his head upright. Without children, he cannot be an ancestor, working with God to provide rewards and punishments for his descendants. Each man deserves to be part of this cycle. And poor Aluel, Magit's betrothed, is fearful of being forsaken in old age with no daughter to cook for her, no son to provide, and no cattle. Woe to the woman alone, for who will sustain her?"

Alier heard only breathing from behind him; the onlookers were held in awful silence.

"Usually the elder brother of one deceased must do his duty by the betrothed, the widow, for it is as if they had been already married. This man's duty is to enter the hut of the woman, to unite with her, so that their child may bear the name of the dead man. Then his family will provide cattle and sustenance for the woman who is otherwise desolate.

"You are the eldest cousin, closest to Magit. It is the wish of his family, and my wish, too, that *you* shall enter the hut of Aluel to fill her with child if God wills. This will sustain the name of your cousin and give status to Aluel. Let it be said that the son of Adol knows his duty, even though he has been among foreigners."

Sometime during this speech Alier had begun to feel a clammy chill run along his spine and the back of his neck. He tried to speak. Words were blocked in his throat. He managed at last to say, "Father, please...I am a student. I am too young—"

"Not immediately," said Adol, lifting his finger for attention and his voice for approval of the listeners. "At the end of this school year, you may take pause for another year and live here, with Aluel. If after a year the woman is barren, it shall be said that it is God's will; man can do nothing unless God allows. In either case, my son, you shall be free to marry another woman of your choice. This is but a limited obligation, you see. For the sake of Magit, whom you loved."

For a time Alier could think of nothing at all, so stunned was he by his father's request. Aluel? To be her husband but not really husband? To be with this woman he hardly knew, certainly had never courted or thought about as a bride of his? Of course, he noticed girls and thought about marriage, but that was far in the future. Had he stayed in the village, he would have married young. Now, in the city, with his thoughts on distant lands, it seemed absurd. Besides, he did not love Aluel.

The hiatus seemed long; in truth it was but a moment or two. Alier caught a single vision in his memory, a vision of peace and hope and love. Melodies came to him, and the chorus of voices in his mind now blended with another sound, quite close. Just outside the hut, in the cattle byre, a lamb was bleating, *"Baaa-aa! Baaa-aa!"* Perhaps it was a white lamb. Perhaps its voice came to him now as a sign.

Alier rose to his feet. He bowed his head and clasped his hands before him "My father," he said, "I would fulfill every duty known to me, except as that duty is in conflict with the will of God. The will of God as I have learned it, and as I feel it in my heart."

Adol leaned forward, squinting as if to see his son better. Everyone in the hut seemed to strain forward, too.

"I have not declared it yet, Father, because I have been surrounded by a conflict of ideas. But I know in my heart that I am a Christian. I believe it is meant for me to follow the ways of the Church. I will adopt a new name, a Christian name, and heed the commandments and rules that the Fathers taught me when I was just a small boy, when you sent me to the mission school to become as much as I could be."

Adol's face was motionless as granite. He stood to full height. The silence in the hut was complete as everyone assessed the possible consequences of his rage.

Alier spoke again. "I cannot do what you ask, Father, because in the eyes of the Church it would be adultery. It would not be a true marriage. Also, I could not then marry another woman. It is commanded that one man marry one woman, that their union is blessed and eternal. If I did this thing, I could not stand up as a man. I could not approach God with a clear conscience. I beg you to understand, Father."

Adol raised his staff. He brought it down on the hard

mud-caked floor of the hut—once, twice. "Leave us," he commanded.

Swiftly the hut emptied except for one man, Alier's uncle Nyong, who rushed to embrace Alier. Then Nyong gently put Alier aside.

"My brother," he addressed Adol, "I understand your consternation. Also, I see your pride in a firstborn son who knows how to reach into his own heart for the truth. Each man must find his own truth when it comes to these matters. Our ancestors have revealed this to us in many ways."

"Indeed," said Alier's father, standing stiffly opposite his brother-in-law. "But what am I to say to the family of Aluel? I have no other son of age to serve her, and how long shall she wait, grieving and childless?"

Uncle Nyong motioned with his hand. Both men sat down on the bed, facing one another. Alier remained standing, silent.

"Aluel, daughter of Yel, is a good-looking woman, is she not?" said Nyong.

"She is good-looking," admitted Adol.

"Her teeth are very white."

"That is quite so."

"Her hips are wide and strong for bearing many children. I have heard it said she does not laugh too much, nor does she spend her days in idle gossip."

"She is a good girl," said Adol. "But what has that to do with our duty? Does she not, with all this beauty and goodness, deserve our help?"

"Surely!" agreed Nyong. "It must be true that many boys would want Aluel for a wife. Nephew, didn't others come to court her? In the cattle camp, was she forlorn?"

"No, Uncle," said Alier, feeling a sudden brightness, a lifting in his heart. "She was very popular; in fact, I went with Magit when he courted her, and three other men stood waiting on the road. Two were from fine families with many cattle, both strong—one a fine wrestler, the other a warrior of note."

"So you see," said Nyong, clapping his hands together, "we must release Aluel from her bond. We can be generous, as befits a chief's family. It shall be said of Chief Adol that he is generous both to his family and to his clan, that he provides for the widow and releases her from bonds that might harm her future. In short, Brother, we shall let Aluel keep the marriage cows your family paid at the time of betrothal. She shall be free to find another man, but she does not go poorly like an orphan. And your son is released from a duty that would surely compromise his faith."

Adol stood quite still, pondering. Then slowly he nodded as he tapped his staff on the ground in thoughtful rhythm to his words. "Five cows were given, as I recall. Strong and healthy beasts, befitting the status of my family. Yes, she can certainly keep the cows." Adol drew a deep breath. "My son can return to his studies and learn the ways of the world. It is good. Let Aluel be free of her betrothal. I have spoken."

And so it became broadcast throughout the village and beyond. It was told at night by the fires. Boys sang about it as they tended the cattle. Aluel was free to marry the man of her choice, and Alier, son of Adol, took a new name, Ambrose, after a saint of the Church.

The name of Magit was remembered and elevated. Six infants born to the tribe that year were given his name.

Another ending, one that was widely told and celebrated in songs: Adol did go with his son to Khartoum, where he stepped into the clinic and was given consultation by a doctor, leaving with a packet of pills that freed his joints from pain and kept him limber. So rejuvenated was he that he visited his young wife frequently and became the father of twins, one boy and one girl. It was a very good sign.

The Secret
Rasha and Rola's Story
NORTHERN SUDAN

EVIL CREEPS ALL AROUND us, like fog and falling rain. But it is not so easy always to find it; sometimes evil hides. Sometimes what poses for evil is goodness, deep goodness within. Listen to this tale of suspicion.

The two girls were accustomed to hearing whispers and to seeing groups of boys and girls darting glances their way. Still, it was irritating. It had been so since they were babies. Twins were always the objects of talk and conjecture. Even adults would comment openly, "Oh, look, that one is fatter; this one is prettier. How do they behave? This one seems more genial, look at her smiling."

Everyone compared them, even their mother. "Be still, be more dainty, like your sister." Or, "Why don't you speak up for yourself, like your sister?"

Only their father, Karim, saw two separate bodies, two distinct souls. He seldom spoke of them as a single entity the way most people did—"the girls" or "the twins" or "the sisters." Their father knew them, it seemed, more thoroughly than anyone. He knew that Rasha needed pretty things; bright cloth and flower petals had delighted her since she was an infant. Rola, on the other hand, would coo and clap her little hands at the sight of the large gray house cat, the strutting of a hen, or the flight of a bird. The two girls were different. But often he sang to them the song he had composed:

"One heart,
My two lovely ones,
One heart of goodness and joy, ah,
May you live long and well in service to Allah!"

It would be impossible to say when exactly the disturbance had begun or which of the girls first noticed that something was wrong. By the time Rasha spoke of it, it seemed that the secret had been sitting there between them like a dark, mute, feathered thing for years. "I do wonder where he goes," she said, rolling her eyes. They were large and beautiful dark eyes. Her father compared Rasha's eyes to a water lily gliding in a dark reflecting pool.

Rola shrugged and pursed her mouth. It was a lovely mouth, with full red lips; her teeth were like beautiful pearls, her father would say, promising that when she married, he would buy her a long glossy strand with a golden clasp. "It is only business," Rola said. "All men disappear on business. We do not need to know about it."

"Well, we know he is a trader—sugar and soap and spices. All the lovely smells we have here," Rasha mused, for they had grown up with these things, and they were most pleasant. "But some men," she said, "have other interests." She frowned. "Perhaps he goes to a woman."

"Be still!" scolded Rola. "What a disrespectful thing to say! He is our father."

"He is a man," said Rasha, tossing her long hair over her shoulder.

"Perhaps he is preparing a surprise for us. Then wouldn't you be ashamed of your suspicions?"

"I am talking about these many months of sneaking away, saying nothing," replied Rasha crossly. "Anyway, we have no special days coming—no birthdays, no festivals."

"Maybe we should ask Mother," suggested Rola.

"Of course not!" exclaimed Rasha. "That would be the worst thing to do."

"Then, we will forget it. We will put our minds on something else."

"We will forget it," agreed Rasha. "We will not mention it."

But once it was out, once their suspicion was put into words, they could no more forget it than one can forget rain or pain or a longing for something sweet.

In the night when the thought awakened her and haunted her, Rola spoke out, "Rasha, are you asleep?"

"No," whispered Rasha. "I heard a door close. Then from outside, footsteps."

"He has left again," whispered Rola. She was already sitting up in bed, now pulling on her sandals.

"Where are you going?" Rasha exclaimed.

"Hush! I'm going to see where he goes."

"You are going to follow him?" Rasha's voice was a squeak.

"How else?" Rola pulled on her shawl, covering her face and her shoulders.

"Wait for me, then!"

"Hurry!"

Outside, the chill damp air made them shiver, and they trembled, too, with excitement—a mixture of dread and delight—for they had never been out alone at night, never on such a mission. Before them at a distance, a shadow flitted up and down, back and forth, as tree limbs and buildings first obliterated, then revealed, the shape of their father, walking quickly and with urgent purpose.

Their father was tall and thin; his face was the color of molasses, a smooth and deep golden brown. The girls had inherited his high color; in fact, it was this quality more than anything else that often brought thoughtless remarks: "A pity they are so dark, Howath, and not favoring you more."

"It is just so," said their mother, folding her hands together and clasping her lips tight. "Still, they are good girls, Allah be praised."

"You must get them married before they are too old, Howath."

"Yes, yes, someone will marry them; never fear."

Now Rola pulled at Rasha's arm. "Hurry! He is going into that alley."

"Wait—my sandal strap—"

"Hurry!" Rola rushed ahead in time to see her father turn as if he had heard something, but just as swiftly she ducked behind a large drum filled with trash. The smell made her gag, but she held her hand to her mouth and waited. From within the drum she heard scurrying. She resisted the impulse to look inside; she would have been pleased to see the family of rodents, how they survived. Instead she now pushed on, with Rasha beside her, panting.

Far down the lane, their father hurried, and the girls had to trot to keep up. On and on they went, seeming to fall farther and farther behind. "I have a pain in my side," Rasha gasped.

"Then, wait here. I'll come back for you."

"You must be crazy!"

"Stop talking, then, and come," panted Rola. "You sound like an old woman."

The moon was drifting downward; the sky was shifting its colors by the time their father reached a dwelling—a poor, tiny house at the edge of town, surrounded by stubble fields, with a rough dirt road leading to its door.

The girls heard a muffled rapping. They saw the door fly open and in the golden glow of lantern light from within, the shape of a woman. She was old; she was tall; and she was very black. Her face was puffed with age; her hair was a cap of gray.

"The woman," whispered Rola, her tone ironic.

"Who is she?" asked Rasha.

"We have to listen," said Rola.

Together they crept closer, and below the small window, they squatted. The walls were a patchwork of crumbling plaster and wood and tar paper, sealed with mud. The window had no glass pane, but thick wooden shutters, which were thrown open, and the girls could hear everything plainly.

"Are you well, my son?"

"Very well; and you, my mother?"

"Well, also. And you walk here to me?"

"I am strong, Mother, never fear."

Rasha and Rola looked at each other. Rola's heart was beating like thunder; Rasha's fingers dug into her sister's arm.

"And your wife, she is well?"

"Very well, thank you."

"And your children—the beautiful girls you speak of with such love?"

"Ah, they are growing more beautiful than ever. What they say of their father, I do not know. Other children talk, spreading tales. You know how it is."

"I know God has sent you to do this work. It is a pity you have no sons to carry on your name and your work."

"God willing, the work will be completed in my lifetime. Then my girls can live in purity, with no blood on their hands."

"Do they know...anything?"

"People talk. Rumors fly. The regime sends out edicts against people like me. Traitors they call us. They speak of policy, 'rightful detention of prisoners.' *Prisoners!* Women and children!"

"If a regime teaches evil, we must fight it in our own way."

"On the other hand, I hear it murmured against me that I deal in human flesh, that I line my pockets with jewels and silver." He laughed slightly, then coughed for a time.

Rola shivered. She often heard her father coughing of late. These long walks in the dampness were not good for his health, she knew.

"So the children know nothing?"

"I do not spoil their childhood with horror tales."

"My son, everyone learns everything sooner or later."

"Let it be later, then."

The old woman laughed. Through the window Rola saw the woman's dark hand, swollen with thick veins, caress her father's face. "So like a parent," the woman murmured. "To spare the child. I tried to spare you, too, as long as I could. Then came the time our people needed you so desperately."

"No need to explain, Mother, or to apologize. I am honored to do this work. It is my destiny."

"Of that I am sure," replied the old woman. "Well, there are some names that have come my way from various quarters. The village of W——, you know about the raid during the last dry spell? Seven girls were captured, all under the age of marriage."

Karim sighed greatly. "The age of my own girls."

"Not all have the means... mostly the parents are poor. I have names, dates they were captured. One is of a grown woman, taken many years ago. Nobody knows whether she is still alive, but her child needs her. And a boy, captured when he was only eight or nine years old. Perhaps he is now gone over to the enemy. We do not know. But we have his name. You can give the names to 'the Man.' He will come soon and try to redeem them, yes?"

"Yes. Tell me the names."

And the old woman began to recite the names. She spoke each one slowly and with force, in the way of one who has never learned to read and write, who needs the impact of voice and breath to penetrate the mystery of what paper and pen can do.

Rola bent down to whisper into Rasha's ear. "She is our grandmother."

Rasha whispered back, nodding, "Yes."

"Should we come out, then, and reveal ourselves?"

"No."

"Our father dare not claim this black woman as his mother. It would ruin him."

Rasha bit her lips, and tears showed in her eyes. "Hush. Hush."

Rola, too, was weeping with regret and longing.

They squatted below the window, arms around each other, locked together. And as they waited thus, the old grandmother spoke the names, "Dabora Achol Amou, Kir Deng, Kwol Biong..."—until the list was done and the woman sat exhausted, as if she herself had captured and released the slaves, as if their burdens were also hers.

Karim repeated each name as he wrote it firmly with a pen on a scrap of paper. Rola saw his seriousness, for his tongue was pressed between his teeth as he labored for correctness. He spoke a good deal about correctness, their father.

Now Karim stood up. From their seat beneath the windows, the girls could see first shadows, then definite shapes, as mother and son touched lightly, hand to shoulder, hand to waist, in an embrace that was more one of spirit/heart than of body.

"Go well, my son. Go with strength."

"I will do my best, Mother."

"Be careful! Oh, so many evil ones are abroad, and looking, looking..."

"They will not catch me!" His tone was light and playful.

"Be careful, still. Take no chances."

"Mother, nobody knows. Not even my family. Do not worry. I am safe."

"Until next time!"

"Next time."

Rasha and Rola remained motionless. The door swung open, causing the air to stir. Karim walked out, and the shadow shapes changed. A bird of early morning let out its cry— Was it of gladness or warning?

Suddenly Karim turned back. "I nearly forgot, Mother! I brought you some..."

"Come away! Hurry!" Rola pulled her sister by the hand, and together they raced across the field, their feet flying, skimming the dew-wet earth, until they reached the lane, then the road. Their thoughts were wild, whirling, their faces steaming from the heat of their efforts.

Twins—one heart, two bodies—each felt the same shame and the same pride.

As they ran, they gasped out the plan that they would follow.

"We can't tell."

"Of course not."

"He could be killed...the regime—"

"Swear, swear to keep it a secret!"

"I swear. I swear."

"He is brave!"

"Our father."

They ran on without speaking, until at last they were back in their house and in their beds. Rasha and Rola lay panting, letting quietness come back into their bodies.

"I am sorry," whispered Rasha, "for thinking bad things."

"I thought it, too," whispered Rola.

"I wish we could tell him," said Rasha.

"We cannot," replied Rola. She knew for a certainty that Rasha would keep the secret, and so would she. Someday, perhaps, when there was peace in the land, when black and brown were brothers, and all recognized that this was so, then they might tell their father about this night, this terrible and wonderful night.

Bearing Gifts
Angela's Story
REFUGEE CAMP, NUBA MOUNTAINS, SUDAN

THE LAMB AND THE CHILD are the same—oh, beautiful lambs! Beautiful children! I sing, beholding you. How quietly you sit listening now. Are you asleep? No? Then listen and imagine angels.

"He is coming, coming for Christmas, the bishop! Truly it is so; we must prepare."

For days in the Nuba Mountains the women chatter and whisper and laugh behind their hands, full of talk and gladness. The child we call Angela watches them, her eyes bright, full of mystery.

Angela speaks seldom, and then very softly, often only to me. When she first came to us, I was the one who picked her up. I wrapped her in a gown and fed her gruel of sorghum and water with a bit of salt. I had no sugar, but then she had never tasted such and did not know better.

As I speak of this, a small yellow bird sits on a twig before me, head nodding. Maybe the small bird knows the truth of what I tell and is in agreement. Our people suffer, yes; and the small bird nods. This child was like twigs and sticks, her belly round and too full—we know this is not from food but from hunger. The child cried not, nor did she murmur. I looked into her eyes, and everything she knew—and even the things she had forgotten—stood in those dark eyes of hers. We called her Angel—Angela—the name that the Sister taught us.

Small yellow bird remembers that time, doesn't it? Many children walking, some with sticks, for they were injured— one with no foot, another with no hand—ugh! Small bird flies away; to hear such is too grim.

This child came walking, too. Someone had brought her out, maybe thrust her into a sack—who knows? Brought her to freedom. But without family, without village folk or any kin, what would become of her? Some folks traveling brought her to us, saying only, "Another orphan." So Sister from the Medicine looked her over.

"Only a babe," said I, but Sister looked into her mouth and felt her limbs and fingers, too, then shook her head.

Sister's face is calm always when I see her, but this time there was a cloud in her eyes and she told me, "Not a baby but a child too small for her age. Much too small. Without nourishment, you see, and without space to run and move limbs, the child does not grow properly. But see this smile, so innocent! An angel."

Now Angela comes to me, puts her hand into mine. "The Bishop is coming," she repeats, whispering the words tight into my ear. "When?"

"At Christmas time," I tell her. "You know the birth of our Lord, don't you? You remember what I have taught you from the Book?"

"Yes, yes, I know," says Angela. With her fingers she traces a design on the side of her face, high, beside her right eye. It is three marks, like scratches but deep—laid there by fire, the mark of a slave. Angela smiles. "He rises again. 'We thought he had died, but it is not true. He lives!' Isn't this what you tell us? That he lives?"

"Yes, Angela. Indeed. In our hearts."

"But the bishop is coming for true, at Christmas time. Will he bring gifts?"

"Gifts," I say. "Yes, surely."

Still she remains close by my side, speaking into my ear. "Tell me again how he bled, and yet he lives. Tell me."

"Yes, they pierced him, and he bled," I say, thinking of the Book and the things I have tried to teach the children, wondering what they understand. And now I see in her eyes a glow that I never saw before. I say, "I have told you of the resurrection." But how does one explain resurrection to a child like Angela? "Do you know what it means, my child?"

Angela looks surprised. Then she laughs. "It means to live," she says, laughing more. "To live again, to come to this place to see me, just as the bishop comes. It can happen," she says. "With faith, anything can happen. You told us this."

She is so young, so innocent. Does she imagine her own father might come to her for Christmas? Is this the resurrection she imagines, the gift she seeks?

"Tell me about your father," I say. Until now I have not dared to ask. Others spread talk about those days. I have heard nothing from Angela's lips.

The small yellow bird has returned. Its eyes glare out at me; it turns its small head, accusing me: What do you mean? How dare you make her remember?

Angela is silent now, her lower lip pulled in, white teeth biting her lip. She nods slowly. "I saw."

"What?"

"Everything. What they did to him. The blood."

The yellow bird flies down, swiftly picks a seed and flies away with it. One small yellow feather is left on the ground, beside the tracks of the bird. Angela picks up the feather. "Bird flies away to heaven," she says. "But see, it leaves something here for us. It is a sign of living still, even when we cannot see him."

I notice something now that makes the breath catch in my throat, hard, like a stone. The track of the bird resembles the mark on Angela's face—three lines connected, fanning out like the toes of a bird. My heart is on fire with hatred, though I have tried not to hate, and I wish to teach the children only love. But I hate the hand that branded this child!

There is no time for hate or for anything except making ourselves ready for the bishop's visit. I have seen him once, at a distance, when he came to bless us and to start our school. Bricks of mud, the color of raw earth it is, to hide from the planes that would roar over in the sky and destroy it. Why do they want to destroy a school? you will ask me. And I will say, Because they do not want the children to learn, to grow—not these children.

One room is where the children learn to read and write. Sixty children sit and sweat in that room, *aiee!* like a cattle yard, full of smells and groans. They speak their lessons, following Teacher, for there are no books or pencils. All eyes follow Teacher; all hearts leap at the thought of knowing, *learning.*

Angela learns with the other children, sitting all day on the mud floor. Sometimes she will sit on a sycamore branch with six other children beside her. When one child moves, the branch trembles and bounces. I have told her about schools in the village, where I was young once and learning to read. There are chairs, I said, and a board where Teacher makes marks for reading. Angela stares at me, laughing, then traces the three lines with her finger. Chairs? Board? She has never heard of such.

Always Angela carries a small pointed stick. With it she draws letters into the earth, writing words, learning.

At night she tells me words of songs they are learning now for the bishop's Christmas visit. The children will sing, "Go tell it on the mountain!" They will sing, "You are like the apostles; you come to bring us Christmas!"

Every day Angela steals away behind the huts. I see her sitting by the ashes of the fire pit, scrubbing, rubbing, polishing something.

I do not intrude; I remain apart. Every person needs a

secret, held close, with nobody watching. My secret is the knowledge that the bishop comes bearing gifts. A new shawl, perhaps, for a woman. Soap and precious salt. A bottle of oil for a man, for rubbing into his skin, making him powerful indeed. For the children, oh, there will be dresses and shirts, and sandals made of tires, strong and beautiful. Angela has never worn shoes. I long to see her small toes in those sandals. I will bind bells to jingle around her ankles, sounding merrily for Christmas!

Excitement blows around us like clouds of dust, thick and rising. Every day more—shouting and calling, learning songs, cutting down twigs and binding them together to make crosses for bringing to meet our holy guest. People come walking from far away—choirs to bring songs for the bishop.

And as it is always, the day that was long and far away comes swiftly so that the morning is a flash of joy—today! We rise with the first cackle of the rooster, never mind to let it draw out a respectable *kray-kree-oodle, kray!* No, we rise swiftly and run to the well to draw water, rubbing our faces and limbs to shine clean.

Angela and I, with our brooms of rushes and twigs, sweep the dirt in front of our *tukel* so that not a hair or a seed, not a scrap or a peel, remains. "We have the cleanest dirt in the land," I say, and Angela traces circles and circles with a small stick to make a pattern. Beautiful! It is Christmas.

We sip water. We eat gruel and some pumpkin leaves. We wait. And then! And then! Bells and drums, everything that rings, bangs, talks, shouts, or sings—all together as it tells in the Book—hallelujah!

And we go, all of us with one step and one voice—men; women both young and old; sons of chiefs; common folk; and, of course, the children, all sizes, all the same in their joy and stepping high.

We have drums made from logs, and coffee cups; we have empty shells that the planes have thrown down upon us. The shells are sent to tear apart human flesh. They destroy our works, the works of our hands, but today we take them and make them into voices. *Brum, brum*—with sticks and pipes and poles we beat the drums that are our voices of joy. It is a fine, loud clatter, and the singing, also, like fifty goats together and a bull to lead them, bellowing strong.

"O come, O come, all ye faithful!"

I hear the gasp from Angela as the bishop approaches, splendid in his white garments, and the red satin cap on his head, and the cross swinging on his breast. Splendid, splendid is the staff he carries, and all the buttons on his gown, and the watch of pure gold around his wrist; ah, if only we had ribbons for Angela's hair! I have put her hair into many braids.

"Where are your ribbons?" I ask her, having saved long for them but not finding such anywhere in the hut.

"Traded them," she says serenely, "for this gourd."

So Angela is plain, with only rags to cover her, but holding this large gourd close to her chest.

If the bishop is tired from his journey, we do not see this in his eyes. They are luminous as stars. His smile fills the clearing with light. The bishop is Sudanese, his ancestors both African and Arab. A true leader of his people, banished now, he returns to tend them. He has traveled far to see us, to baptize babies and make marriages and to bless us and to bring us Christmas.

Angela and I stand together, watching our people being blessed, when overhead comes the roar we all fear. People murmur to the bishop. He stops, head tilted to see the sky. Bombers. They come to bring us terror on this Christmas Day. What shall we do? Bishop, tell us, where can we run?

"We will stay here and hold our Christmas Mass," says the bishop. His voice is like a mother's song, gentle but strong. "We will move under the trees. The leaves will cover us."

Quickly, quickly, we move under the trees. The leaves arch over us, making a chapel of green with golden sunlight shining through. In a moment we could all be scattered, some of us dead. Not one baby cries. Not one person moans. In silence we listen as the bomber circles, circles; and in this deep silence, there is a strange sense of peace among us.

In silence we stand. We listen. The plane roars past, leaving its helpless tail of smoke, slinking away like a hyena without its prey. I want to laugh and shout; I want to wave my arms in joy. We pray now, with a new passion.

Then it is time for gifts! I see the large satchel carried by the bishop's assistant, a tall thin man with light hair curling like small new leaves. His eyes are light, his face is round, like a full moon. He takes long steps, stiff in his walk, as is the way of white people.

Angela laughs a little; she has never seen one like this before.

We stand in a line, waiting, singing, while the bishop

blesses and speaks and gives gifts to the people. Some get a kiss. Some a hand on their head. Some he murmurs over, others he gives a smile. We wait, Angela and I, wanting anything that he has to give us. From the satchel come dresses and sandals, pants and shirts, a hat or two, scarves of many colors. Children and men and women find their gifts, wave them with delight. New clothes are put on over old—hats onto heads, shawls around shoulders, pants on top of rags—and everyone smiles. My heart is filled with longing; I want nothing for myself, but for Angela, everything.

We wait and we wait and suddenly it is we who stand before him, caught in the glow from his eyes. I tremble. The air is warm around me, some flame burning into my heart. I want to sing and shout, but all that comes from my throat is a whisper and I drop to my knees. I bow my head and murmur, "Bless this child, Bishop; she saw her parents slaughtered before her eyes, and then she was enslaved."

Both the bishop's hands come to cradle Angela's face. With his fingers he traces her scars, and then . . . and then he presses his lips to the brand, and I cry out for happiness. He loves her! Of course he loves her.

He points to the long white man with the moon face and the light hair. "What would you like, my child? A dress? Perhaps some sandals and a blanket to keep you warm?"

Angela does not move. Her eyes roll first to the clothes, the sandals, the blankets, and then to the gourd in her hand.

"I have brought *you* a gift," she says, giving him the gourd. She has carved out a wide round opening. She has scraped out the flesh and made it smooth for carrying water. Water here is life, nothing less. The outer shell gleams from her rubbing, and scratched into the surface, blackened with coals from the fire pit, are the words GOD WITH US. Words here are the future. Only with words will we be free. Beside the words, stuck on with sap from the trees, is the yellow feather of the bird.

My heart sings. I know now that Angela understands everything I have tried to teach her. I wonder whether the bishop sees in this gourd the things Angela knows of life and freedom and resurrection.

The bishop takes the gourd into his hands. He gazes at it in silence, studying each symbol. "This is a treasure," he says. "Thank you. Now choose, my child, a dress, a blanket, shoes?"

Angela's gaze moves from the bishop's face to the tall white man, and she points. The bishop turns. He gazes at the assistant. Thrust above his ear is a yellow pencil.

"You want the pencil?" asks the bishop. His brow is furrowed.

"To write," says Angela. "To learn."

The bishop nods. "Give it to her," he says. "Give her the pencil."

New dresses flutter in the breeze; colors seem to flow together. Humbled now, the people clasp their hands together. Children stare in silence; women kneel.

Do the others see it, too? A tear flows from the bishop's eye, leaving a smooth, soft trail on his cheek. He whispers, "You are the lambs. You are his lambs, indeed."

Small Things
Marcus's Story
WESTERN UNITED STATES

Marcus felt the changes in his classroom. Maybe it was the stories. Somehow the world was coming closer to him; Africa did not seem as far away as before. Perhaps he was the one changing, he thought. He was part of a team, an army fighting oppression.

Now when everyone sat on the rug, Marcus sat between his friends Colin and Jason. Together they worked at writing letters to celebrities, telling them about the enslaved people in Sudan, asking them to help.

Marcus had written a letter to their congressman, explaining about their cause—what Miss Hazel called their "two-pronged attack." They would raise awareness and also raise money for redemption. But the congressman had not replied. Most of their letters were never answered.

"We're not giving up," Miss Hazel would say firmly. "We are made of steel."

There were some successes. A newspaper back east did a long article about their class efforts. Afterward Miss Hazel got letters and e-mail from kids and teachers all over the country, and even as far away as Japan. Dozens of classes were following their lead, writing letters and raising funds. It was exciting to know they had started something big.

Miss Hazel put pictures of African children all along the walls and the bulletin boards. Twice a week after noon recess, everyone assembled on the rug for a meeting and another story.

As Marcus listened to the stories, he studied the faces of those children. Sometimes he imagined that they themselves were speaking. He could almost hear their whispers: "Help."

One morning there was a letter addressed to Marcus, care of Miss Hazel's class. It bore the seal of the United States Congress. When everyone was settled on the rug, Miss Hazel, her eyes shining, handed Marcus the letter.

"You open it," she said. "Maybe you'll want to read it to us."

Marcus read the letter aloud, repeating it over and over in his mind afterward. "'Dear Marcus, please tell your teacher and your classmates that I will be happy to visit with all of you to discuss our mutual concerns about freedom for the enslaved people of Sudan. I congratulate you on your efforts to become personally involved and to make a difference. I look forward to meeting you...'"

All day Marcus felt as if he were flying. Everyone congratulated him, talked to him, made him the center of things. Never before had he been what Miss Hazel smilingly called "the man of the hour."

After school that day, Marcus stayed to do his homework. No longer a punishment, it had become routine. After school Miss Hazel would pull up a chair and sit beside him, speaking softly, encouragingly. She showed him things he had never known before about math problems. He really liked fractions, splitting numbers into bits and putting them together again.

Marcus set to work. Now that he understood what to do, it was like completing a puzzle. He liked the feeling of control.

Marcus heard voices out in the hall, first low, then rising and angry.

"What makes you think that you are making any difference here? I happen to know that some very influential people condemn these activities. They say you are actually encouraging slavery by offering money to slaveholders—"

"Now, now..." It was Mr. Grundy, the principal. "I'm sure we can straighten this out. I'm sure Miss Hazel has the best of intentions."

Miss Hazel's voice was strong and clear. "The children refuse to sit by and watch passively while other children are being enslaved. They're taking action, and I'm proud of them!"

"Now, now, Miss Hazel, I'm certain Mr. Warren has some valid points to make. We must do our best to listen to the concerns of our parents."

"Mr. Warren, the children are learning so much through

this project. They're writing letters to our congressmen and senators, to the president—"

"I don't think children need to be taught to criticize the government."

"Now, I don't think Miss Hazel intends—"

"I know exactly what Miss Hazel intends! She is using our children to become a national celebrity! Oh yes, you want your fifteen minutes of fame. Well, let me tell you, you're not going to get it at the expense of my son!"

"Mr. Warren, I couldn't care less about being on television—"

"I send my son to school to learn the basics, not to get all worked up about a bunch of primitives in Africa who have been fighting and killing each other since time began!"

"I'm certain we can find some middle ground here," came Mr. Grundy's voice, cracking a bit.

"There is no middle ground," Miss Hazel cried out, "between slavery and freedom!"

Doors slammed. Feet pounded. Marcus sat at the desk, unable to focus on the problems or on anything except the echoes of Miss Hazel's voice ringing back at him. He had never known anyone like Miss Hazel before. She would sit quietly beside him, watching as he worked on his math problems or English grammar. And they'd also talk and talk, not only about the slavery project but about everything. He'd help her answer letters and file papers and even answer e-mail on the computer. Lately he had become her main helper, but nobody called him a kiss-up or anything. Actually, it was cool.

He asked her once, "Do you have any kids, Miss Hazel?"

She had smiled very broadly and said, "Yes, I sure do. Two wonderful kids, both in college now."

Lucky, lucky kids, Marcus had thought to himself, and then he felt lousy for thinking she might be a better mom than his own. He wanted his mom to be the greatest, but his mom was always so busy and so tired, sometimes even too tired to come to him and say good night. She'd be in her bedroom, lying down with all her clothes on except for her shoes, looking at the ceiling, and if Marcus came in to see her, she'd look over and say, "Hi, there. Excuse me; I'm bushed."

Now Marcus looked up as Miss Hazel came into the room, her eyes red, face flushed. His mom used to look like that often when she was with Dude. Miss Hazel held a handkerchief to her nose, then turned to the windows. He heard her sigh deeply.

"What's wrong, Miss Hazel?" Marcus asked softly.

"Nothing. Well"—she turned to him, blinking—"I have this condition. Sometimes it makes me—it makes my eyes sting."

"I have a condition, too," he said softly. "At home."

"I know." She nodded and laughed slightly, even as she wept. "Some people want me to stop talking about problems, you know, like slavery." She leaned against the chalkboard, shaking her head. "What am I supposed to teach if I can't tell children the truth about the world?"

"Maybe parents think we're too young to know," Marcus said. "They think we're stupid. Like, my mom used to tell me things I knew weren't true, like, that she and Dude were going to get married, or that he was going to get this great job and we'd move to San Francisco and be this real happy family. I knew it would never happen."

"Where is Dude now?" Miss Hazel asked. She put the handkerchief back into her pocket.

Marcus shrugged. "I don't know and I don't care. I hate him."

"You do?"

"I don't know. I'm just glad he's not around."

"Me, too," said Miss Hazel. She smiled. "So you're the man of the family now."

Marcus was surprised. "Yeah, I guess so."

"What are you planning to do?" Miss Hazel asked.

"I guess I'll help you clean the board and go on home," he said.

"I mean," she said gently, "with your life."

Marcus took a deep breath. "I don't know."

"When I was your age," Miss Hazel said, "I decided to be a teacher."

"I don't want to be a teacher."

"Then, don't. I just meant...you could be thinking about it."

"I want to do something that takes me places," Marcus said, "like be a pilot or a conductor."

"Lots of different jobs involve travel," Miss Hazel said. "You might look into it. If you were to learn a foreign language, you might work for the government or join the Peace Corps or work for a company that has offices abroad."

"What's 'abroad'?" Marcus asked. He felt dizzy—important and small all at the same time. He had never imagined such things as the teacher now set before him.

"*Abroad* means 'other countries.' I love to travel. I'd love to go to Africa," she said, "and see the people—people so different from us but still, much the same."

"I feel bad sometimes," Marcus blurted out. He hadn't meant to say it.

Miss Hazel's gaze was steady, patient.

"I mean, terrible things are happening to those people in Sudan. Like the stories you tell us. All they want to do is be alive and go home to their families and we—well, I get so mad at my sister sometimes, I just want to get out of the house." He stopped, breathless. "It makes me feel like—I don't know. Bad."

"I think I understand, Marcus," said Miss Hazel. "Those kids in Sudan are fighting for their lives. By comparison it makes our problems seem very small, and then we feel guilty."

"I guess so," Marcus murmured.

"But our problems are real, too. Others might be worse off, but we still have our own worries. Right? The important thing is that you care."

"Right." Marcus nodded. He felt flooded with feelings, warmth mixed with a lingering sadness, as if he might start to cry. "I'm getting a bike soon," he said. "I'll go up to the mountains with it, and I'll ride it all over town."

"That sounds terrific," Miss Hazel said. "My son used to ride his bike all the time. He loved it."

He lowered his voice, though there was nobody around but the two of them. "I found this baseball card," he said.

"It's real valuable. I went to the mall last week to trade it in, but then I didn't do it. The catalog says the card is worth at least two hundred dollars. The man at the store thinks I'm stupid. He offered me fifty."

"You didn't take it?"

"No. I don't like being cheated."

"I don't blame you, Marcus. It isn't fair. You have to know what you stand for."

"How can I tell what it's really worth?"

"You could ask several places and compare," said Miss Hazel. "Or have your mother go with you."

"She wouldn't," he said. "She's busy. She works all the time."

"Maybe I could go with you," Miss Hazel said.

"Would you? Really?"

"Sure. If your mom says it's okay. I guess I'd need a note from her. You never know what might get some people upset."

Miss Hazel gathered up her purse, notebook, and jacket. She stood at the door, waiting while Marcus got his backpack.

"Good-bye," she said as always. "Take care."

"Take care," he replied.

He turned back. "What are we going to do if they make us stop raising money? How are those kids going to get free?"

"Nobody can stop us, Marcus," she said. "We're determined, made of steel. We're abolitionists. Right?"

"Yeah." Marcus ran home, wishing his mother would come home from work early. He couldn't wait to tell her about the congressman and the letter and everything that was happening at school. He'd tell her about the newspaper drive they were planning, to raise more money for redemption. Miss Hazel said they needed parents to help pick up newspapers. Maybe this time his mom would help. Maybe if she got involved, she wouldn't be so tired and so unhappy; maybe she'd make new friends and have fun.

Marcus heard her key in the door half an hour early. He let out a yell. "Mom! Wait till you hear what happened." He ran to meet her.

Her face looked strange, her eyes dark and piercing. "I need to talk to you, Marcus, and if you lie to me, I swear, you'll be grounded for a year. Did you or did you not ride with Paul on his motorcycle?"

"Mom! Please, I...I was with Serafina. I thought it was okay."

"A cop came to work today," she said. She pulled off her shoes and tossed them down. They hit the floor with a thud. She sat down on the sofa, where Marcus slept, where his pillow and blanket were still in disarray. She faced him, her eyes blazing. "How do you think I feel when a cop comes to talk to me and all the customers are staring, looking at me as if I've committed a crime?" Furious, she gathered up his bedding and threw it aside.

"How do you think I feel when they tell me that my daughter is hanging around with a bunch of hoods who go to the mall to steal every other day, and that *you went with them!*"

"I didn't steal anything!" Marcus shouted.

"Don't you raise your voice to me! You went on that motorbike with Paul."

"Yes, I went to the mall, but—"

"You disobeyed me, didn't you? You knew I'd never allow it. What do you think is going to happen to you, hanging around with guys like that? As it is, the cops want to talk to Serafina about her 'associates.' Get that, *associates*! And now, you. Isn't it enough that I've got Serafina to worry about?"

"Why are you yelling at me when it's Serafina you're mad at?" Marcus cried. "You let Serafina do anything she wants. You let her get away with everything because she won't let you boss her around anymore, and I'm not going to, either!"

His mother leaped up and she grabbed him, standing. He flinched and backed into the wall, his heart beating wildly, his hands up before his face.

His mother drew back. "You are grounded for a month, Marcus. You are to come straight home after school every single day. I will phone to see that you're here. And if you disobey me . . ." She stopped, sat down on the sofa again, eyes straight ahead, as if she were speaking to someone in authority. "I am not going to go through this with you, too. Not again. Once is enough. You are not going to start down that path, I promise you. I will not let it happen."

The memory of his day was ruined, his joy like so many old scraps of paper. Marcus thought of Miss Hazel and her children, how she probably sat down with them after school and they all talked and had a snack together. He thought about Colin and his dad collecting baseball cards and Beanie Babies. He thought of Jason, whose family all went for long bike rides on Sundays.

All *he* had was a mom who was always tired and angry, and Serafina Skunk.

The Lucky One
Aziz's Story
NORTHERN SUDAN

EVERY BOY WANTS TO become like his father, isn't it so? Yes, Father is the keeper of clan ways, protector and teacher. Wisdom comes from the father's mouth, and justice is in all his deeds, isn't it so, children?

"So you will come with me today, Aziz, yes?" his father asked jauntily, as if it were a sudden, new idea, as if Aziz hadn't been pacing and panting, waiting for the day to arrive. Not that he had never been to the city before. Naturally, he had gone with his mother and *amah* many times, to shop or to attend the medical clinic for some childhood ailment or other. But he had never gone as the son of his father, to be introduced to his father's associates and workers as "my oldest son, Aziz; may he follow in my footsteps."

The other men would look him over. They would smile their approval and clasp his arms and speak praises. "A fine boy, Ibraim; he looks like his father. Tall for his age, isn't he?"

"He is a good son, obedient and hardworking," his father might say. Aziz lived for that moment. And it was fast approaching!

Aziz had a quick breakfast of bread and fruit—some figs and dates, and apples dipped in cinnamon. His mother, mindful of the importance of his day, hovered by Aziz, as if she might touch his hair or his face, give him endearments to take away with him. For this day was as much an initiation as any could be.

"I will take Aziz when he is near ready to work with me," his father had declared—not once but often. "I do not want him to shame me with childish questions and childish ways."

Now nearly thirteen, Aziz was ready for secondary school. Swiftly the years would fly. Aziz would move into his father's many commercial holdings—a large shop in Khartoum, a wholesale plant of which Aziz knew little except that foreigners invested money there and drinks called cola were sold in bright bottles. Then there were the fields and the herds that Aziz knew about vaguely; a gentleman spent little time among peasants and animals. That was for slaves.

Slaves surrounded Aziz. They took care of his little brothers and sisters. Females washed his clothing, mended his sandals or took them somewhere until they miraculously reappeared, looking new. When he was a small child, slave women bathed him and trimmed his nails and rocked him to sleep if he cried. The stone walls and the paths of the compound were maintained by slaves. They also tended the flowering vines and the vegetables—spinach, maize, okra, tomatoes, and onions—which made fine, fresh fare for his family's table. Slaves dug wells and repaired fences and carried heavy loads. They scrubbed the tile floors of the house and cleansed the windows of the clinging sand that blew from the south.

Aziz's beautiful mother kept her hands smooth, rarely touching water. Aziz knew she had a special female slave to bathe her and tend her hair. Sometimes there was a sharpness between the two; the black woman would retreat, cowering, wailing as if under blows, though Aziz had never seen his mother strike a slave. Sometimes when he was in his room, he heard things. The sounds triggered his imagination so that he shut his eyes tight against the awful visions, pinched himself into silence, and finally fell asleep.

They are not like us. This was a fact of life, not learned, exactly, but known just as it is known that the sun rises each morning and the stars come out at night. It was simply an observable and obvious fact: *They are not like us.*

"Aren't you ready yet? I am leaving immediately!"

His little brothers were pouting and wailing, "Why does Aziz get to go? We want to go, too!"

"Not this time," said their father. "Go now; *amah* will take you out to play." To the *amah* he called, "Take them! Keep them happy. Their mother does not like to hear all this crying."

Aziz ran out to the car, where a driver waited, his face impassive, eyes straight ahead. Aziz's father was not one to laugh and joke with his servants, although it was said that he could be generous if someone especially pleased him.

They drove through the compound, with its winding roads sheltered by leafy trees and flowering shrubs, out to the main road, where the traffic of people and animals, wagons, carts, and an occasional truck created a clatter and chaos that made Aziz's heart leap with gladness. He couldn't wait to see the world. His parents, protective and worried, had kept him too long in the compound. Out here, people screamed at one another in mock anger. Swiftly they melted into smiles and praises. They bartered, they begged, they chanted and scolded and laughed out loud. Aziz loved the sound of it, the life.

While they rode, his father either gazed out the window or spoke softly to his assistant, who sat in front with the driver. The assistant twisted his body around to meet Ibraim's gaze. Every few minutes the assistant turned away, rubbed the back of his neck, and arched his back, then swiftly sprang around again, attentive to Ibraim's questions: "And did you send them a second notice, and what did they say?" "Do they know we have a firm delivery date?" "Why hasn't the second shift filled its quota? You must look into it." His father spoke softly, unlike other men of wealth who shouted and threatened.

Aziz listened, feeling lifted up with pride. When the car pulled up in front of a row of shops, people drew back and ducked their heads in greeting. A woman shooed her little children aside. A vendor of vegetables beamed and bowed and called out, "How goes it, Ibraim! Greetings to you, and blessings; it is a fine day when you appear, my friend!" Everyone knew his father; everyone watched Aziz. Men smiled and clapped him on the back, now that he was almost a man.

Ibraim brushed past them all, nodding, acknowledging their words, speaking softly. The shop was filled with wares—cloth and trinkets, bottles of oil, crates of onions, mounds of soap, bags of grain and sugar. As Aziz and his father entered, three dark men with dusky eyes rushed forward, nodding and bowing as they came. "Master! Glad to see you today!" One came with a shuffling gait, holding his side. All were dressed in shirts and denim pants. Nobody could say that Ibraim did not treat his slaves well. Aziz often saw others with holes in their clothes, some even going naked.

His father gazed about with the keen eye of a professional, a manager. Nothing escaped him. He pointed to a large box of nails. "These must be sorted," he said. He looked behind a small tower of crates. "Someone has failed to sweep the floor," Ibraim observed. He made a quick gesture with his finger. "These jars must be properly stored. You. We are sending a lorry, which must be loaded at once."

It was all smooth and swift and professional. Yes, that was the word, the word they used at school. *Professional.* "You young men will become professionals; it is important that you learn proper speech, proper dress, proper attitudes."

"Come into the back room, Aziz." His father walked with long strides. Aziz followed, and the three black men came behind. Several crates stood under a wooden work table.

"Pull them out," Ibraim directed. And then he nodded to one of the slaves. "Open it. Careful!"

The wood made a cracking sound as the slave opened the slats with a long metal wedge. Aziz drew closer. His father pushed the slave aside and looked down into the crate. Aziz felt his father's hand on his back, a slight shove. "Look. What do you think of that?"

At first Aziz saw only packing material, then the polished butt of a rifle, the dark stock, the trigger. He turned to his father, wordless; he felt suddenly taller, powerful—and bright as if he were lit from within. "Father! Father!"

"It is a small but profitable portion of our business," his father said softly, earnestly. "You must learn all of it, Aziz. I am counting on you. Someday you will be the master of the family operations—the compound, the stores, the factories—everything. Today we are only going to a few places, scratching the surface, so to speak, and you will get a feel for how things are managed. Little by little, Aziz, you will be put in charge, and as you fulfill your responsibilities, you will be given more." His father stood back, arms folded across his chest, smiling. "Now, what do you have to say for yourself?"

Scarcely breathing, Aziz said, "I would like to see the rifle. I would like to hold one, please."

His father laughed indulgently, bent down, extracted one of the rifles, and handed it to Aziz. "Careful. You must always assume the worst—that it is loaded, that it might go off."

Carefully Aziz lifted the rifle so that the butt touched his shoulder. It was heavy, and it smelled wonderfully of oil and polish. Aziz squinted through the eyepiece. He felt the trigger against his finger. In his imagination he was a hunter of wild animals, a magnificent hunter envied for his stamina, his marksmanship, his keen mind, and his gracious manner. Everyone envied him, Aziz, son of Ibraim.

"Come now, we must pack up and be on our way."

The three slaves had retreated, their eyes downcast. Now Ibraim motioned for them to bring the crates out to the lorry that stood outside. "Careful! Careful!" Ibraim urged the men. One stumbled against the doorjamb and let out a swift, fearful cry. "Sorry, Master!" He sank to his knees. "So sorry; I am careful, see! How I step carefully now!"

Ibraim brushed the man aside, his eyes and mouth set in a look of contempt.

The slave lifted himself, head still bowed; he was sweating heavily.

Outside, Ibraim spoke to his assistant. "I want that man sent to the fields tonight. He is too stupid to work indoors. Let him clean out the goats' pen."

"I believe he was wounded in the side, Master."

"The goats will not worry about that," said Ibraim, laughing. He turned to Aziz. "Do you want to ride in the cab of the truck?"

"Oh yes, thank you!" Aziz ran and climbed up into the truck. The driver, a heavyset Arab, whistled constantly between his darkly stained teeth. They drove some distance without speaking, following the black Subaru in which Aziz's father rode. At last the truck slowed. It lurched over a rutted strip of dirt road approaching a field with two half tents. The field was dominated by a very large maple tree, its pied bark and flickering leaves making a tapestry of color against the dry, dusty earth.

At first Aziz did not see the people, for they sat quietly under the tree, camouflaged by their dark skins and ragged clothing. Then Aziz saw movement. Their faces turned. There were several children, among them a girl about his own age. The children's eyes were very wide, the whites like pure cotton, the black of them as dark as coals.

"What are they doing here?" Aziz asked, half aloud.

The driver grunted. "You will see."

His father had alighted from the car and stood tapping his foot, calling out to a man, who came running holding a small notebook against the front of his robe. The white *gallabiya* on his head and his white *dishdasha* were both peppered with dust from the road. The man looked harried. Now under the tree there was a slight shifting, and Aziz saw several black slave women standing over the children, who sat silently as if time and place meant nothing to them. All seemed frozen in their expressions and in the static postures of their arms.

Aziz glanced at his father. Ibraim gave a slight jerk of his head, motioning Aziz to come and stand beside him.

"Moamar, this is my son, come to join me here. Now, as we agreed," his father said, nodding pleasantly, "two crates, sixteen pieces in all. You are welcome to count them."

"It is not necessary," said the trader. "Everyone knows that to do business with you is to deal with an honest man. Of course, things must be done properly. I have here a bill of sale for the *abeed*. A girl and a man, as you requested."

"Which are they?"

"The one in the front, with the colored cloth over her head. We call her Fatima."

"She looks small, not yet ready for a man."

"Look again, *Sayed*. She is nearing womanhood. You want them young, do you not? Better that way, to train her to your own desires."

"Yes, yes. Do not talk to me like a salesman, Moamar. We made a bargain, and I will keep mine. What about the man, then? What is his disposition? I need a strong one to take charge of my cattle, especially the bull."

"He is a hard worker, Ibraim, and strong. See for yourself." The man called out loudly, cupping his hand to his mouth.

The slave was brought over. The chains made a scraping sound as he shuffled his feet, being unable to lift them more than a short space above the ground. Aziz gazed at the black man. His eyes were focused straight ahead.

Ibraim said, "Lift your arms."

The slave did so.

"Are you injured in any way?" Ibraim turned to the trader. "I do not have the time or the resources to spend on medicines."

"He is in good health, as I told you, *Sayed*, excellently strong and a fine worker. He will tend your animals or build you a road; he can do the work of two men, and he eats but little."

"He understands our language?"

"But of course! He speaks perfect Arabic. He has been with us since he was a boy of eight or ten. He understands everything. And he knows what is expected of him. He has been trained in the way of our faith; he knows that he has but one road to heaven and but one way to survive in this world, and that is to obey his master."

Ibraim drew closer to the black man. He looked into his face, reached out and pressed the man's back and his biceps, then bent down to examine his legs. Ibraim turned once again to the trader. "What is his name?"

"Abdulla," replied the trader.

"Kwol," said the slave. "Kwol Biong." He focused his eyes directly upon Ibraim, a flash of defiance.

For a moment the air seemed rent, as if with a rifle shot.

Ibraim pursed his lips, thinking deeply. A quick gesture brought the assistant to his side, holding a stout club. Ibraim seized the club. He raised it high above his head and with it struck the black man across the back and shoulders—each blow measured, each making a terrible, sickening thump— six mighty blows.

Aziz wanted to scream out, "Stop!" but his throat was paralyzed.

Ibraim tossed the club away and stood back, breathing heavily.

"I am so sorry, *Sayed,*" babbled the trader. "I have not known him to be insolent in the past. I apologize, truly."

"Never mind, it's no matter at all. Better that he learns immediately who is the master here and how to serve him. I will have no heathen working for me, with heathen names." He spoke to the slave, to his face. "Your name is Abdulla."

Aziz felt a strange terror starting in his fingertips, a numbness, and a kind of flashing dread before his eyes. He was sweating. His belly felt too full, unsteady. The slave had not moved or cried out at the beating, but now Aziz saw how his teeth were clenched together. His entire face was a grimace of pain. For a moment Aziz saw the man look up at Ibraim, his father, with a look so full of hate that it made Aziz tremble and call out, "Father!"

But his father misunderstood the cry and touched Aziz on the shoulder and said softly to the trader, "See that the man is put into the lorry, and the girl, too."

There was a small commotion from under the tree. Aziz could not make it out at once, but then he became aware of a moaning and a thrashing sound, which billowed and rose to a wail, the cry of an animal when it is roped and is to be slaughtered momentarily.

"Don't take me; don't sell me, please; don't take me away. I will do anything, Master; leave me with my sister. Take us both! My sister! My sister! Let us stay together, I beg you; I have nobody. Please, please don't take me."

Aziz was terrified by her screams. He wanted to beg her to stop screaming. There was only one outcome; she had been sold. Her purchase was complete. Now it remained only to determine whether she went mute like an animal, or whether, by resisting, she called his father's wrath down upon her head.

The girl's arms and legs flailed, and still she screamed. "Don't let them take me, Sister—my sister! Please!" In the next moment his father's man had reached her. It took only a few seconds for him to grasp her arms and bind them together with rope, to thrust her down on the ground, to bind her ankles and sling her over his shoulder like a sack of grain or an animal that has been felled.

As the man strode past him with the girl on his back, Aziz saw her eyes. For an instant she and he were locked together, a look of amazement and agony. Had there been a moment longer, the mere span of an extra breath, he was certain he would have spoken to her. But what could he have said?

Aziz heard the thud of her body as she was thrown into the back of the lorry. And now Aziz turned to the others under the tree, and he saw their faces. They no longer seemed identical, except in their impassivity. Only one young girl reacted, gasping for breath, beating her thighs as she held back sobs.

Aziz watched as his father's slaves set down the rifles in their crates at the feet of the trader.

"Peace," said Ibraim, nodding. *Sallam Alleikum.*" He motioned to Aziz.

"*Sallam Alleikum,*" murmured Aziz.

"A fine-looking boy," said the trader, beaming. He cast a sidelong look at the open crate, at the rifle showing, the wood so smooth and sleek, smelling sweetly of fresh oil. The man's hands itched to hold that rifle, Aziz knew, but he continued to nod and smile his praises. "Takes after his father, I see—a tall, fine boy, ready to work beside you, is it?"

"Yes, well, in due time," said his father. "This is his first excursion with me. He learns fast, this one."

Aziz stood beside his father. Dimly now, he heard the

sounds from under the tree. He felt the blazing heat against his cheeks, the strength of the hot sun smiting him on the chest. His mouth tasted as if he had eaten tin.

His father and the trader exchanged gestures of friendship and farewell, hands together, then lifted almost palm to palm without really touching.

"Be well."

"You, too; go with God."

"All good things to you, Brother. Let me know when you wish another transaction."

"Yes, yes, surely."

Aziz followed his father to the car. He did not want to look into the truck, but his eyes seemed drawn by a will of their own. He saw the black man sitting against the hot metal, his gaze steady but unseeing, and he saw the girl lying down on her side, wrists and ankles still tightly bound. Her flesh was beginning to swell around the tight cords. She had drawn her knees to her chest, and her arms were curled around her knees in the same way his little sister slept when she was exhausted. But this girl was not asleep. Aziz knew she was not asleep, for her lips moved in some silent mantra, continuous. He looked away.

"Do you want to ride in the truck, Aziz, or in the car with me?" asked his father.

Aziz could not speak. Something seemed to choke him. To ride in the truck with those two people, tied and beaten like cattle, no. He could not ride in that truck, so close to their pain. But to ride with his father—this man whom he had idolized all his life, who now had changed before his very eyes into someone he could not recognize—this seemed impossible.

"Come on, Aziz! Do you want to stand here forever? Come on with me, then. We'll go together."

Only in his mind did Aziz answer: *Together? No, I will never go with you. I would rather die.*

At home his mother greeted him with eager questions. "How was the day, my son? Did you please your father? Did your father teach you much?"

Aziz gazed at his mother. He did not speak. His little brothers were wailing and pouting, "What did you bring us?" "Did you bring presents?" "Lucky Aziz, always gets to go with Father."

Aziz only shook his head.

"You are exhausted," said his mother. "Go and lie down. Have a rest, my dear. We can talk about it later."

But Aziz knew there would be no talk. What he didn't know was how he was going to live out the rest of his life. In the dim twilight of his own room, he lay down on the bed, and looked up at the ceiling fan that whirled endlessly. In rhythm, soon the words came to him. *It is a lie. It is a lie. They are exactly like us.* And then he knew: Someday he would say those words out loud.

The Way of the World
Dabora's Story
NORTHERN SUDAN

THE SADDEST THING OF ALL, children—hear me! The saddest thing is not even to dream. If they can destroy our dreams, we are lost forever.

She lay there staring at the stars, those points of brightness in a vast black sky, and she repeated her own name in her mind: *Dabora Achol Amou.* Over and over again she said the name, as if it might erase the name *he* had forced upon her, the way he had also forced himself.

"Your name is Hawa," he said. The new name made a sharp sick sound, like spitting out phlegm. "Hawa, do you hear? You will answer to this name only, or you will be sorry, I promise you!"

He always kept his promises. Like the promise that, before he took her into his home, he would "take care of her," make

104

her acceptable. He had taken great care of her indeed, fought to subdue her, first with his fists and feet, then with threats of a knife. He dragged her to the hut of the old woman— the surgeon—who was known for her craft, respected and feared. He secured the help of two other men, for Dabora was strong. She had screamed and struggled. It was useless. The old woman waited, her small knife sharp and poised, until Dabora lay motionless, with a rag in her mouth and cords holding her arms and legs, tied to posts.

Dabora remembered screaming once, a cry that terrified even her. Then everything had faded until she was revived in the master's house, on a mat on the floor by his bed, like a dog. "Now you can be my extra little wife," he had said in a rumbling, purring tone, like a wildcat, sly, waiting to leap. "As soon as you heal a bit, Hawa, then..."

The name Hawa sounded like a curse in her ears. Always it preceded a command—to fetch water, mind the goats, scrub the floor, scrape the droppings from the henhouse, bathe Master's children, wash his clothes, even his hands.

He does nothing for himself, she thought with contempt, re-membering her own people, how they worked. Her husband, Madut, had glowed with pride when he completed their hut and the cook fire and the cattle byre. He cut his own wood, gathered stones and laid them up for a wall. He made a road leading from his house to the house of his uncle and to the cattle byre. Oh, how he longed for a truck, a tractor, to do the work better. He would tell her, "Dabora, one day when this war is ended, when the difficulties are no longer, I will have a truck. I will help build up this land, wait and see."

His arms and legs were strong; he was like a bull, leaping, dancing, with bells and bangles on his wrists, spears poised to strike the enemy in mock battle, splendid to see. With the other men he was strong and magnificent; with her, gentle. Oh, the songs he composed, singing of their life together, his pleasure of her. "Your teeth are white as milk, yea, like purest white ivory..." At night he whispered his songs to her, and he told stories of his brave deeds as a lad; he filled her with joy and pride, and he said her name in a way that no other ever did, "Dabora." On his lips her name sounded like the rustling of streams, the stirring of leaves.

Sounds intruded. Scraping, shuffling, a stifled cry. In the darkness Dabora Achol Amou could make out stumbling shapes. She heard the harsh command: "Go to sleep! In the morning we will deal with you—I promise you!"

"I have no place. I have no cover."

A sharp sound: flesh against flesh, a slap. "Now, that will keep you warm. Be silent!"

Dabora Achol Amou—the name was meant to bring her comfort and lull her to sleep. But now her ears were trained to the sounds of this other person's breathing, the soft, muffled cries. The person was young; she could tell by the stirrings. A girl, perhaps the age of her own daughter. How long had it been? Dabora had tried to keep count of the years, but it was not possible. Every day was a workday, nearly every night a summons, if not from her master, then from an-other—his relatives or friends. Soon now, they would leave her alone. Her belly grew heavy with child. She had seen, with others, that when this was so, the men turned away. It was her one small reward, after all this time of chaos, to be left in silence in the nights, to look at the stars and whisper her name to herself: *Dabora Achol Amou.*

But now, here was this young one sniveling and turning, scattering leaves and debris. "What are you doing?" she called out, sharp. "Digging a hole like a stupid weasel?"

"I . . . I—who is there?" The words were in Arabic; the tone was that of a child. "What do you want?"

"I only want you to be still. Who are you? How do you come here?"

"I am Fatima."

Dabora wanted to laugh and spit out her contempt for the name—*you and ten thousand others!* They were all named Fatima, all the slave girls, after some myth their captors knew, a fantasy.

"How do you come here?" Dabora repeated, whispering. If Master heard them speaking together, they would be whipped.

"My new master brought me. I came in a truck," Fatima said with a slight ring of pride. "Master has loosened the ropes now," she said, rubbing her wrists and ankles. "It is good."

Dabora raised herself on one elbow. By the light of the moon, she could see the girl, bronze skin, straight hair, and the whites of her eyes—the whites of her eyes, cloudy—not like the people of Dabora's race, but mixed.

Mixed. The word brought a fluttering, choking feeling to her throat. It was how her baby would also be, all the bright blackness rubbed out of her skin, the twist gone from her hair. She would be that halfway color, noncolor, the light creamy skin that was prized among the captors, and now even among the captives themselves. Weren't they told, day after day, that black is evil and ugly? Some would look upon their own black hands, their own black feet, and despise them.

"I am Dabora Achol Amou," she said in a strong voice.

"What sort of name is that?" inquired Fatima.

"It is my name," she replied. "My own. It is from my people."

"What do you mean? Are not all people the same, either *abid* or master?"

"No." In the darkness Dabora frowned. "Why did he bring you here?"

"I do not know. I am his," she said simply.

Dabora felt a terrible sense of annoyance. Ignorant girl! It angered her unreasonably; the girl was like a beast in the field, unaware of any life around her, except to serve, to eat, to exist.

The girl spoke again. "He traded me for rifles."

"Ah."

"What am I to do here? Will this new master tie me to the fence, as the other one did?"

"He is no better and no worse, I suppose, than all masters," said Dabora. "Go to sleep. You must be tired."

"But...but I am...cold."

"The night is not cold."

"Always I was with my sister. We slept together, close. Now I will never see her again!"

"Where is your mother?" asked Dabora, knowing the question to be cruel but needing an answer.

"My mother was sold long ago. But always I had my sister."

"Come here. Let me look at you." Dabora rose to her knees, squinting to see the girl. She was not a young child but on the verge of womanhood. Tiny buds of breasts showed through the thin weave of her white dress. Dabora's heart lurched, though she tried to harden her thoughts against the girl.

"Well, how did you come to your last master in the first place?" she asked. To keep the girl talking would warm her a bit, stop her tears and the rustling, then Dabora could get some sleep.

"What first place? Always I was his."

"Always? You mean, born to him?"

"We were always his, in his household, me and my mother. I knew my mother only a short while. She is gone now. I do not know where. But it does not matter. Master is the one who gives us food."

"Born a slave," Dabora murmured. "You have no memories, then, no dreams—"

"'Memories'? 'Dreams'?" The girl gave a laugh of confusion, a childish laugh. It was good, in a way, to hear laughter again, and Dabora smiled in spite of herself.

And Dabora clutched her memories ever more closely. In the night, those memories wove themselves into her dreams so that she never forgot her name or her past. Her hair was wild. She had no beads or bangles or pretty things anymore, nothing except the one dress that would soon fall from her body in pieces. The skin of her hands grew dry, like the hide of a goat. Still she sang her soft silent song in her head. *I am Dabora. Once I was beautiful. Once I was free. I shall be so again.*

In the days and weeks that followed, new paths opened up before Dabora. Mornings, though filled with demands and curses, were not utterly bleak. There was this girl, Fatima, looking at her, asking questions with her eyes, needing guidance. As they worked, Dabora whispered stories recalling the wedding of her sister; the cattle camp days when she went with her brothers far from the village; the beautiful, starry nights.

Fatima listened. She never asked questions but only murmured, "So, so," like a child hearing a legend of long ago.

The two slept close together at night, huddled against the wind. By day they shared a spot of shade. Occasionally their hands touched, and Dabora remembered the touch of human flesh, the sweetness of it—of mother, husband, child.

Sometimes she and Fatima laughed together, as when they were tending the goats and a small one came bleating, butting its head against their knees, looking for food. Food was another thing between them. The table scraps that Master tossed out, these Dabora salvaged and picked over, giving Fatima her share. Often, seeing the girl's thin arms, she gave her an extra bit of pumpkin flesh or a grain cake, saying, "Take it. I have enough."

"You must eat for the baby, also," said Fatima.

"No, it is unwise to grow too fat, unhealthy for the child."

"Is it your first?" Fatima asked. They were alone in the hills, finding grass for the goats, looking out for predators—

foxes, hyenas, wildcats. It was hard work, harder than the household, but in a way less taxing, for there were no masters to scream and scold and fling objects that could bruise and pierce.

"My first, a daughter," said Dabora, "is at home in my village, God willing, in my own land."

Fatima's face lit up with interest. "What is her name, this firstborn?"

"Amou is her name." It had been too painful before to share this. Somehow Dabora had needed to keep Amou to herself, safe in her heart.

"Who cares for her?" asked Fatima. "Is she grown? Is she married?"

"She is a young girl, like you."

"Where is her father?"

"Hush! I'm sick of your questions! Look, now, that goat is running toward the edge of that cliff—quick! If it should fall..."

Fatima rushed over, catching the small goat in her thin arms. She picked it up, held it close against her chest, nuzzling its head with her chin. "I would like to have a child," she said.

"It is almost certain, someday you will," Dabora said dryly, and she held her hands to her belly.

"I mean a child that I could keep. My own."

Dabora gazed at the girl ready for womanhood but so small as to be pitied. Lack of food and lack of freedom had stunted her. "Yesterday," Dabora said, "I went with Master into town, you know."

"I have been to town, also," said Fatima, "the day they brought me here. It was very full with people, all sorts, and I even saw a bus. It was scary, let me tell you, with stinking gas and a roar. Did you see a bus?"

"Bus and cars and marketplace, I saw all this," said Dabora, "and a man—an Arab with dark glasses over his eyes so that one could not see into his heart. I was standing by the booth stacked high with cloth—brilliant, beautiful colors of cloth, such as my mistress buys and wraps around her body, so."

"Have you owned such a cloth ever?" Fatima asked, her eyes wide.

"Yes. Two times, a new piece of cloth with colors. Yes." Dabora felt the skipping of her heart—a joyous, fluttering feeling, like the skipping and leaping she had felt at the market just yesterday when the man called to her and beckoned, his fingertips barely moving, slight as the turn of feathers.

"This man spoke to me," continued Dabora. "I was scared, let me tell you, to be seen talking. But he stayed very still, and I took two steps back while my mistress was bartering— you know how shrill she can raise her voice, like a hyena in the night."

Fatima laughed. "A sick hyena!" Then she asked softly, "What did the man want?"

"He asked my name." Dabora's breathing came heavy now. "I told him, 'Hawa.' He said, 'No, your true name. What is it?' I told him, 'Dabora Achol Amou.' He asked me, 'Are you paid for your work?' I told him, 'Only with blows and scraps from the table, and this growth here in my belly.'"

"What if Mistress had caught you speaking with this man?" Fatima asked, trembling. "You must not do this, my friend. Please! They will beat you—or worse."

"Well, I spoke," said Dabora. She folded her arms across her chest, head high. "I spoke, and I told him I am captive. I am forced to work and to...to please my master as he wishes. And the man said...the man said..." Dabora turned over her shoulder, gazing sharply all around. "He said, 'If you want to be free, you must come to this place in the night.'"

"'Free'? A 'place'? What can he be saying?" Fatima cried out, her fingers at her lips. "You must not listen to such as this! He is an evil one, come to turn slaves away from their masters. It ends in evil, Dabora, do you not know this?"

"I know that I cannot remain so," said Dabora fiercely. "This child, it is mine! I have a right to this baby, don't I? If I remain here, Master will take it from me. When will I ever see my baby's face? Kiss his small fingers? I am going, Fatima. Only one question, one wish, remains. You must come with me. Will you come with me?"

Fatima shrank back, shivering as if she had seen the ghost of her grandfather, hoary and bent and striking out to slay her. "No! No! How can you imagine such a thing, Dabora? They will find you. They will punish you, oh, terribly."

"I will be skillful," said Dabora. "But if they find me, let them kill me. I would be dead and away from this misery."

"And then? When death comes? Do you think you will find a place in paradise, having disobeyed and fled from your master, whom God placed over you?"

"God placed me under nobody's heel!" cried Dabora. She clasped Fatima by the arms and gave her a shake, hard. "I was born free. You—what do you know of freedom? You and your people, forever owned, like cattle—"

"I belong to my master!" Fatima cried. "He feeds me. He gives me water. He is strict, but that is the way of the world. Look," she said, speaking in a whisper now, "I knew a woman who fled her master. They caught her and tied her, high, to a tent pole. Her hands swelled up. For days she hung there, not daring to cry out, for if she did so, they beat her with sticks. Silent, then, she hung, and her hands began to swell and they began to stink, and when they cut her down, she was useless, without hands to work, and crazy from suffering. This one was no longer useful to her master. He cast her out. She was sent into the forest. Maybe eaten by wild animals, who knows?"

"A terrible tale," said Dabora. She shuddered. The sun was turning down, low. "We must bring in the animals," she said. "Hurry." And as they walked, herding the goats, Dabora spoke once more. "We are not like these animals," she said. "We are meant to be free."

"We are free to serve our masters," said Fatima. "It is our choice to obey or to be punished."

"No!" cried Dabora. "A slave has no real choices at all. Fatima, don't you see? We are not animals, to be owned by another."

"God has placed us so," said Fatima. "It is the way of the world."

That night, lying down on the ground, Dabora kept her eyes wide open, staring at the stars, whispering her own name over and over again to herself. By and by, as the moon rose high, she stood up and brushed herself off. If only there were water so that she could wash herself! One does not wish to step up to freedom in filth.

She sighed deeply, then moved toward the shape of the young girl, folded into herself in sleep or, perhaps, pretending.

"Fatima," she whispered. "Come. We will go. I have stolen a file and cut a hole in the fence. For this alone Master would kill me. It is no matter now; I must go. Come with me."

No response—only deep breathing, very deep.

"Fatima, I will take you under my arms. I will care for you. We will go to this man. If we fail, let them kill us. It is better to be dead than to be captive! Fatima, listen to me; I know what it is to breathe the air of freedom. It is beautiful beyond anything you ever knew! Come, and we will pray to God; and if he is good to us, we will go home to my village. We will be free."

Silence... only silence from the girl.

Dabora bent down and pressed her lips against Fatima's forehead, feeling the dampness there. "Farewell," she whispered.

In the darkness, Dabora crept through the hole she had dug between the wires she had cut. Outside her master's compound, her heart leaped wildly with a mixture of fear and exultation. No matter what the next moment might bring, for this moment, at least, she was free.

Forever Kin
Majok's Story
REFUGEE CAMP, NUBA MOUNTAINS, SUDAN

EVERY CREATURE HAS ITS PLACE in the grand design, and each must be respected. Still, we must learn to face new dangers; we must grow with the world.

The airport at Nairobi was filled, as usual, with all kinds of people. Their patterns of dress, language, and body movement still fascinated Majok, as if this were his first glimpse of foreigners. He had lost track of his travels, which began when he was just at the age for initiation. Instead of receiving the tribal cuts, he had been chosen for education and sent up north, then to Cairo, and finally to the United States.

Majok loved flying, loved the sound and tremor of the silver planes, huge birds that bore him to lands his ancestors had not even imagined.

116

He moved out into blazing heat, carrying his duffel bag, mentally comparing Nairobi with Westwood, California, where he now lived in a two-room apartment. At night he worked at the library on his book and then, worn out and yet stimulated, he walked the streets, looking into shop windows at the jeans and jackets, computers and other office machines. He was a natural with machines of all kinds; everyone said so. If anything needed fixing in the apartment building where he lived, it was Majok who came immediately, his tools all neatly stored in a box, ready to make repairs.

If only he could repair his people. The thought nagged at him constantly.

A man rushed up to him, wearing a business suit, looking harried. "Ah, your plane was a bit early, Majok Biong; forgive me for not meeting you at the gate."

"Quite all right," Majok assured him. The man spoke a poor Arabic, the only language they had in common. They exchanged the required greetings, inquiries as to health, family, business. As soon as was reasonably appropriate, Majok posed the question. "When do we go? Today, I hope."

"It is a small plane," the man said apologetically, "and we must wait for instructions. It is no small thing, you must realize, to accomplish a landing in the midst of hostilities. The pilot is nervous. He is afraid to be bombed by the northern army; every day they sweep the skies. He is afraid. I have to talk encouragement to him."

Majok reached into his pocket, pulled out his wallet. He had prepared himself with plenty of cash, all in twenties to prolong the counting. Now he slowly peeled seven bills from the stack. "Go to the pilot," Majok said soberly, "and give him this for further encouragement. I must leave today. This afternoon."

"If this is possible," the man stammered, "I do not know..."

"It is a three-hour walk to the camp," Majok said sternly. "We should land late this afternoon, just before dusk. I will then be ready to leave at dawn, before the great heat, to go to my people." There was a slight catch in his throat at the words *my people*. He had not seen his kin for five years.

Five years was a very long time, long enough for him to graduate from university and become a teacher while completing his studies. *Long enough,* he thought, *to be healed from homesickness.* But that afternoon as the small plane dipped down over the vast, varied land that was Sudan, Majok felt a burning in his throat and stinging in his eyes. He blinked away the tears. A Dinka man does not cry.

The landing was treacherous. The small plane lurched and swayed, its engine coughing and groaning, so that Majok was tempted to offer his services should they have any time on the ground for repairs. But clearly the pilot had no intention of staying on the ground longer than it took to dispose of his passenger.

"Quick!" the man shouted. "Run! I leave now. *Sallam Alleikum!*" he blurted out, then revved up his engines and took off.

There was a small committee of greeters, five men from

the village, dusty and lean and looking somehow ravaged. They rushed up to Majok, calling his name, smiling. They clapped him on the back and the shoulders, touched his clothing and his hat, which matched his fatigues, and especially admired his boots and his watch. The watch, a Seiko with an impressive number of dials and digits, winked from his wrist like a huge eye.

"Ah, it is good you have come, Majok Biong. Your father and all your relatives are expecting you. They rejoice at your coming." "Was your trip pleasant?" "Did you have food to eat?" "Are you well?"

"Very well, and your families? The children? The cattle?" Majok responded.

"Ah, then, you must come into the shade and drink water. You must lie down in the shade, and we will talk."

Talk continued until the moon rose high and the stars offered broad portals of light across the night sky. Majok thought that never in all the world had he seen such exuberant beauty and at the same time felt such a well of grief. For the men spoke to him now, without ceasing, of the troubles; of the land once so rich now spoiled; of the huts and cattle byres burned down and demolished; of the rivers polluted, schools destroyed, hospital buildings collapsed under the constant hail of shrapnel bombs. But the worst—the worst, of course—was in the tearing of the people, their very lives lost or limbs blown off by the bombs, and the orderly cycle of life completely disrupted.

"Of course we try," said the elder, "to rebuild ourselves in the camp. It is difficult. The land here is arid. Our sorghum crops do not grow. They bring us strange large seeds of corn, and we try to cultivate them, but without hoes, and in soil full of stones, it is hard."

Majok nodded gravely. If only... if only he had been able to bring something meaningful. They were destitute. He could see it in the faces of the men, their weariness apparent even now in the softening moonlight. Their clothes were in rags. Nobody had sandals or water bottles, or even a rope or a peg.

"What of the cattle?" Majok asked.

"Mostly gone," one man replied. "When the soldiers came, they carried off what they could. The cattle, they terrorized and rounded up. Those that fled, they shot. Our storehouses of grain, carried away or smashed and burned. We have a few cattle, however. By the grace of God some were spared, and we are indeed rebuilding our herds." The man lifted his head; his eyes gleamed. Majok felt a flash of deep, searing pride.

"And the evacuation? How did you choose the camp?"

"It is quite simple," said the elder. "We marched until we found a place no man on earth would wish to inhabit. It is the driest, the hottest, the most filled with rocks and snakes. Here no enemy would seek us. This is the place we camp now, waiting for peace."

"How many are there?" Majok asked reluctantly.

The elder held up his hands, flexed his fingers several times, indicating. "Many. Too many. On the trek," he said, "two thousand died."

"*Two thousand?*"

"Mostly children and women. Some belonging to your father. All of us lost someone." The man shuddered slightly, then bore himself up, shoulders high. "It is God's will. And now you are here. God has sent you. We are thankful."

The burden, the exhaustion, the anxiety, melted down together, and before he realized he was asleep, Majok awakened to the coarse call of a lone rooster perched on a limb, twitching its head as it crowed, long and loud.

"Good morning. You rested well, yes?" Warm tea was ready, and sorghum porridge. Almost wordless, the men ate. Then tersely they picked up their few possessions, one of the men insisting on carrying Majok's duffel bag, and they set out over the powdery, rocky soil, ever inclining toward the refugee camp.

It was June, the middle of the season of *ker,* which children and adults alike longed for and relished. Light rains would transform the barren, arid landscape into a paradise of green and gold, with new grasses and flowers carpeting the ground. Minnows, frogs, crickets, and all manner of insects and birds would fill every space with swift movement and screeching song. It was the time when the cattle were taken out to the cattle camp, when boys and girls spent their days tending their beloved herds and their nights singing, dancing, courting, eating meat until they were full and lazy and fat. As a child Majok had gone with his cousins to the cattle camps, luxuriating in the sights and sounds and smells of *ker.* Even now he sometimes dreamed of those delights and awakened with mixed feelings of joy and loss.

This year Majok had felt an overpowering inner summons

toward home. He had heard, of course, through various agencies and news items and a rare phone call from Africa, how bad things were for his people. Raids were commonplace. Bombings were a terrifying fact of everyday life. And slavery, that age-old African curse, had reappeared with all the evils and cruelties of which man is capable.

As Majok trudged onward with the others, he found himself gasping and taking long drinks from the water bottle slung at his hip. He was getting soft. In times past, he could walk for days without feeling the stress. And it was hot here in the mountains, with none of the blessings of sweet rain or greenery. Even the weather was betraying the Dinka, it seemed.

Under his father's leadership, the clan had migrated nearly a year ago from their village, here to the high mountains where they might be safe from attack. In his mind's eye, Majok still imagined his home, the neat huts with their thick and perfect thatch roofs, the cleanly swept dirt paths, and the children playing, mothers nursing, cattle being tended so diligently by the strong young men who flicked their wrists and stepped high with pride and sang as they labored.

It will not be the same, Majok told himself over and over, while sweat poured down into his eyes and his legs began to ache. *Do not expect it to be the same.* Still, when the guides pointed to the settlement, Majok's heart pounded with dread and disappointment. Hardly a tree or a shrub sprouted from the dry, cracked earth to provide a bit of shade. The single building of ragged cinder blocks had its roof half torn out. A shed partially covered with ugly green paint and topped with

a tin roof was the only visible sign of commerce amid the un-
even rows of huts and the listless crowds of people who sat in
the blazing sun, waiting, waiting for something that seemed
forever distant.

Under a scrap of a tree sat a multitude of children, all
ages, their faces turned toward their teacher, who led them in
singsong through the alphabet. Majok gazed about. Several
men leaned on poles; they were missing legs, blown off by
shrapnel. One of the children, Majok now saw, had but one
arm.

Majok felt a hand clasping his arm. The elder said, "Your
father, Biong, waits. Here is his hut." And the man led Majok
over, walking with slow but purposeful steps.

But there on the path stood a woman, first seeming
strange, and then in a rush she lifted her head and opened
her mouth in a long, wide wail of welcome. "My son!"

"Koj! Koj Magok!" Majok said.

His mother stood with her head thrown back. She was tall
and had always possessed a full figure. Now her breasts hung
flat as leather against her chest; the flesh of her arms shook
with her gestures, hanging loose upon her bones.

Swiftly Majok embraced his mother, repeating her name
over and over.

She wept on his shoulder. "Oh, my son. Oh, my son."

"Come, Mother. We must not stand long this way." It was
an embarrassment among their people for mother and son to
be seen in obvious affection.

Koj drew back, but there was no mistaking the joyful
gleam in her eyes. Majok was not her firstborn. The first son

had vanished twelve years ago, when Majok was only a small child. Since then she had borne three daughters and, lately, another boy.

Koj waited discreetly outside as Majok entered the hut. His father, Biong, rose from his mat of rushes. "My son."

"Father."

They embraced, then sat together and the talk began. First the greetings and physical matters of health and recent happenings.

"Your sister Nyanjur is soon to be married."

"That is good news, Father, if the bridegroom is worthy."

"A good family; a strong young man," said Biong. "We have few of these. Nyanjur is lucky. Have you seen your mother, Koj Magok?"

"She waits outside, Father."

"And your other mothers? They all wait for your return. You must not offend them."

"I will go to them immediately when we are finished talking, Father."

The smoke from the small fire was making him drowsy. Now, somehow, it did seem that he was at home in the village in the fine large hut of his father. A strong sense of déjà vu overcame Majok; his father's voice, the heat of the hut, the mention of the names of his kin made it seem as if he had never left.

Majok listened intently as his father spoke of the tragedy of their village, the destruction and the deaths, the long trek to the refugee camp and the life they were now living—waiting for water, waiting for food, waiting for peace.

"All we hope and pray for," concluded the father, "is to be able to return to our homes. We want nothing—no charity, no help to rebuild. We will rebuild with our own strength. If only there be peace in the land. If only we can go home again."

"What do you do here, Father?" Majok inquired, glancing about the hut. It was swept clean, with utensils neatly lined on the storage shelf, the bed raised well above the ground to ward off insects and crawling things. The thatch, however, was sparse. Back home, Majok knew, his father would have been ashamed of such a roof. Here, it was plenty; it had to suffice.

"I attend to the affairs of my people," Biong said almost sternly. "They come to me still for counsel, with problems of marriages and sickness and disputes among kin and neighbors." He glanced toward the back of the hut, where the family spears were positioned. They were the symbols of chiefdom, handed down through the generations. *If I were not a modern man now,* Majok thought, *the spears would be mine someday.* "You know how it is," said Biong. "The chief must know how his people lie down and how they get up, what they think and what they need."

"I remember it well," said Majok with a smile. Many were the hours he had sat with his father under a tree in their village, listening while Chief Biong dispensed advice and wisdom.

A flash of his new life in Westwood—the classrooms, the library, the streets with their traffic—almost made Majok laugh aloud at the contrast. As if to intercept his thoughts, his father asked, "Have you found a wife, my son, among the Americans?"

"Not yet, Father," said Majok. "I have been very busy, you see, studying and teaching. Besides..." He did not know how to explain it. The women he met were usually students. Some were frankly awestruck by his physique, his blackness, the texture of his hair. "You are so *exotic,*" one young woman had breathlessly told him. "I hope this doesn't offend you, but... tell me—I hear your people take several wives. Is that true?"

"It is true," he had said. This matter of polygamy always excited them.

"Well, how do you relate to those other wives of your father? Isn't there...um...a feeling of...competition?"

How could he possibly explain in a few moments the friendship, the protection he felt when he was among these women? "They are all my mothers," he had said, smiling in spite of himself. "I love them."

"When I find the right woman," he said now, "I will bring her home, here, to you, my father."

"Well spoken." His father sighed, resting his hands flat against his bare knees. "We must discuss a matter of some importance," he began.

"Let it be spoken," said Majok.

As if on cue Koj Magok entered, bringing several slices of dried pumpkin and some nuts on a small woven plate.

"Leave us, woman," said Biong. "This is serious talk now."

"Then I will listen with a serious heart," responded Koj Magok.

Magok held his breath. His father did not brook insubordination from his wives, not even from Koj, the first and highest.

"It concerns family matters," Biong said at last. "I suppose you might as well be informed. But I warn you, do not cry and wail. I have no stomach for it."

Koj nodded and backed away, sitting down with her legs folded beneath her.

"I am growing older," began Biong.

This is a bad beginning, thought Majok. Such declarations were always followed with demands on the young.

"When I am gone, who will be chief? Who will keep the people following the manner of our ancestors? Who will clarify and guide and arbitrate?"

Majok sat very still, biting his lip. *Who, indeed?* He spoke. "Perhaps Uncle or Cousin or—"

"My line," said Biong sternly, "my seed, my son only must succeed me. My son must continue or why have I lived? I would be like a tree, burned down to the root."

Panic began fluttering in Majok's breast. He felt his scalp prickling. Words flashed through his mind: *Impossible, impossible that after all this time my father expects me to come home, and not even home but to live in this miserable camp and learn to minister to a people who neither read nor write nor know anything of the world beyond!* Panic almost made Majok leap to his feet and cry out, but respect and long habit held him still.

"You have a brother," declared Biong, "a brother long lost to us but still remembered. Kwol, your older brother, who was captured by the Arabs long ago, is still in our hearts. He lies in the heart of your mother, Koj Magok; I hear her weeping still."

At this a long sob broke from Koj's throat. Majok did not move but sat facing his father, while the long sounds of his mother's grief poured over him, filling the hut as if with a tangible substance.

"We know that your brother has been among the Arabs, that he was first taken to Khartoum, then to the border. And while I have made inquiries now and again, we have no knowledge of his whereabouts. When one has no direct knowledge, one must rely on signs. Such a sign has come to me lately, Majok. You see, I knew you would come. And I knew the reason for your coming was this: to find your brother, Kwol."

Majok let out a gasp, lifted a hand, was immediately silenced by his father's stern look.

"In a dream, I saw a large basket in the road. I approached this basket. Your mother, Koj Magok, was walking just behind me."

Majok heard an intake of breath from behind him, nothing more.

"I lifted the lid of the basket, and there I saw a snake. The snake gazed at me, then slowly, slowly it crept from the basket and onto the road, where it lay at my feet, outstretched and without menace. Suddenly three small snakes emerged from this larger one, and the three wound themselves around my ankles as if to hold me there. And when I awakened I knew you would come home to me for consultation."

"And the three snakes, my husband?" came Koj's high voice. "What did they portend?"

"Three men," said Biong instantly. "I and my two sons. It is clear that the large snake was a messenger, telling me that all three live—I, Majok, and our firstborn, Kwol. All three will be united. Now we have seen the return of Majok, and I know it is only a matter of time until Kwol will be standing here in this hut and he will take his rightful place as Chief, learning by my side in these last years remaining to me on earth."

Majok sat dumbfounded. "Father," he began, "you honor me that you believe I have the ability and the contacts to find Kwol. I am only a teacher. I live far from here. How could I possibly undertake such a search?"

"There are ways, Majok," Biong said, as he sat up straight, his features firm. "If a man desires a result, he finds the means. You understand the use of modern machines. You speak languages of other peoples. You have learned who is to be paid and who is to be courted with compliments, who is to be won with threats and who with promises. I see that you are a fine, strong man—handsome—and you carry yourself with great dignity. What I ask of you is not impossible. It may be difficult, but the son of Biong, since his youth, never turned away from difficulties. The son of Biong always brought pride to his father, even to his entire clan."

Majok sat in silence; he felt raw from emotions—anger, indignation, love, and longing. Oh, if only it were that simple to provide his father with an heir, to bring back his lost brother!

His mother's sobs now accentuated the dilemma, and even as she sobbed, other females came creeping into the hut—two, three other mothers, all weeping softly, all the wives of Biong. Majok's emotions skidded from irritation to amusement to sheer helplessness; his father had played him well, "pushing all his buttons," as the Americans would say.

Majok stood up now for the first time since he had entered the hut. He stood facing his father, his gaze directed to the back of the hut where the ancestral spears lay, one in the shape of a leaf, the other in the shape of a lance. And as he gazed, he was struck with alarm, for there on the oiled leather beside the spears, a giant puff adder lay coiled, and in front of it, a gourd filled with melted butter.

"Father! Father!" he cried out. "Look there, that snake!"

"Indeed," Biong replied calmly. "Last night it appeared. You see, my dream was a sign. Events happen together, in threes—the dream, the snake, your arrival."

"But, but . . . it is dangerous and poisonous, Father. What if it goes free among the people? Someone will surely be bitten. Such a bite is fatal, especially here, with no medical help. We must kill it, we *must*. Or, if you will not destroy that snake, let it at least be taken away, far away. There are helpless children outside and even . . . cattle it could bite and kill."

Biong went to the back of the hut. He stood gazing down at the puff adder, which reposed on the leather, sleepy and quiet, as if contemplating its buttery meal.

"The snake and we," said Biong, "have long been connected. We are kin. Forever kin. It happened in ancient time that a pact was made between us. How can I kill my brother? How could you ask such a thing of me, my own son, my flesh?"

"Father, these are dangerous times. Sometimes a sign is not what it seems."

The look on Biong's face was thunderous. Swiftly Koj Magok broke in. "Chief Biong! We sent this boy to school so that he might learn. He returns to counsel with us, and he is right. The snake carries much poison; it is a large, large snake. However, as you say in your wisdom, it is our brother and we must not do it any harm. Now, a lorry brought our son home. It is still on the road. Perhaps in your wisdom you will decide that the snake must be moved, taken by the lorry to a distant place, perhaps a place with water and shade, so that our brother snake may find himself in pleasant and safe conditions. We would explain that this is done not by way of rejection but only for its own protection, for if it were to remain here, the snake could be trampled by cattle, who knows?"

All this was said so quickly, so sweetly and earnestly, that Biong stopped still, and even while Koj still spoke, he began to nod slowly. And when she had finished, he proclaimed, "Let the diviner be brought immediately—and two men with long forked sticks and a net."

One of the young wives ran out. In a few moments the hut was crowded with others. The diviner, a woman called Angeth, quickly determined that it was a good thing, not a bad thing, for the snake to be moved, as it would be done with love and protection, and this would be carefully explained to the snake.

"In addition," said the diviner, "let a lamb the color pattern of this snake be brought, and let it be sacrificed in the snake's honor. All will be well."

After a brief scramble, an explanation, and swift movements of sticks and nets, it was done. The snake reposed in the back of the truck. The lamb was brought and swiftly slaughtered, its blood allowed to run onto the ground, with appropriate prayers and songs given by the crowd that had now assembled. "*Thithiey! Thithiey!*" Praise God! Praise God! came the cry from the assembled people.

After some time, pieces of roasted lamb were distributed in appropriate sequence. Majok ate hungrily. He wiped the succulent fat from his lips. He sipped a long draft of milk from the gourd his mother had brought.

"So when will you begin this quest?" asked Biong, tossing aside a long rib bone.

Majok sighed, patting his full belly. He shook his head at the nature of things. Here and now, in his very self, the past and the future were tied together. Omens and signs must meet with methods and machines. He had heard a rumor about people coming secretly to Sudan to buy back slaves that had been captured in raids. They were Americans and Europeans, people of conscience. Majok had thought the story mere propaganda for their organizations. But maybe there was truth in it.

"Tomorrow," said Majok. "I will begin tomorrow to inquire of officials in Khartoum and in America and in Europe.

If there is any power on earth that can find my brother, it shall be done."

"I knew you would not disappoint me," Biong said.

Two weeks later, back in Westwood, California, Majok was speaking on the telephone to a man whose voice was weighted with responsibility and trust. Yes, he had been making his way secretly into Sudan to redeem slaves.

The man assured Majok, "I will still redeem as many slaves as I can. I will fight to abolish slavery. I have pledged to do this. What is your brother's name?"

"Kwol Biong," said Majok. "Chief Kwol Biong."

"I will let you know. The rest is up to God."

Majok's colleague from the office next door came to chat. "What's new? Did you have a good time with your folks? How was your summer?"

Majok grinned and gave him the high five. It felt very good to be back.

Small Things
Marcus's Story
WESTERN UNITED STATES

Miss Hazel had her clipboard out. She was making plans. "So we'll all stay after school next Thursday," she said. "I think we can raise several hundred dollars. If you need someone to pick up papers at your house, write your name on this list and we'll make arrangements."

Marcus groaned.

"What's wrong with you?" Krissy asked.

"I'm grounded," he whispered. "I can't come."

"It's a school project!" Krissy said. "Your mom will understand."

Marcus shook his head. "You don't know my mom."

Miss Hazel pointed to them. "Are you two paying attention? Or is this some private high-level conference?"

People giggled. Marcus laughed, too. How could a person

feel awful and OK at the same time? So many new things were happening to him. Last week Miss Hazel had tacked his math paper to the bulletin board. On it was a yellow sticker of a smiley face and the score: 100%! When he told his mom, she just said, "That's fine, Marcus. But you're still grounded."

Something had shifted at home in the past week, since the blowup. He had heard all about the police and the intervention by social services, his mom and Serafina screaming about the hearing they had to go to. His mom had to take a day off from work, which made her even madder. After the hearing, the two of them had launched World War III in the living room, right over the sofa, so Marcus had no place to retreat. He had to stand there with the two of them, their anger raining down around him.

For a while they just yelled, and Serafina cursed, and his mother looked so furious that Marcus was frightened. Like all fights, it rose, it ebbed.

"You lucked out this time," his mom finally said. "If that social worker hadn't intervened, you'd be in juvenile hall."

"Don't be ridiculous, Mom," Serafina said with a sassy smile as if she had an audience. "Nobody gets busted for just knowing a thief."

"You were an accomplice," his mom cried. "You knew about it all the time."

"I'm not their keeper!" Serafina screamed. "Why do you always pick on me?"

"Obviously I haven't picked on you enough. I haven't been able to get through to you that if you hang around with losers, you lose. If you don't improve, Serafina, you're going to end up in jail, or worse. God knows, I've tried every way I know how."

"Oh, you feel so sorry for yourself. Why'd you ever have kids?"

Finally they slowed down. The screaming settled. His mother looked pale and exhausted. Serafina was slumped on the sofa; his mom stood at the counter, pulling canned goods out of a sack, banging them down on the table.

"Well, I won't need to pick on you anymore," Mom said. She opened several cans of vegetables and poured the contents into a pot. "From now on you've got your own probation officer to report to every month. Now you'll have to report to someone else, someone who doesn't even love you, who won't stand for all this...chaos."

Marcus stood motionless, astounded. He had not heard the word *love* in this apartment, ever.

"And you'll have a job to keep you busy after school and weekends."

"How am I supposed to know how to be a waitress?" Serafina demanded, more softly but still sullenly.

"You'll have to figure that out, and I'm sure you will. You can do anything when you put your mind to it, Serafina. I know you can."

Serafina's eyes suddenly filled with tears, but she turned away quickly, clenching her fists under her chin. Marcus saw her trembling. She was scared and lonely; he had never known that about her before. He wanted to say something encouraging, but he didn't know what.

They sat down at the table, without talking. Marcus felt like he was in a bad movie. Things never seemed to get any better. Often at night, before he went to sleep, he dreamed of heading on his bike for the mountains. He'd put it into high gear, wind along the bike paths higher and higher until he could see the tops of many mountains and feel the fresh wind on his face. He would stand there and yell out, "Hello! Hello, down there," and his voice would echo back and he would finally feel free.

They picked at their supper, some kind of stew his mom had slammed together. It was OK, but mushy. Marcus mopped it up with the heel from a stale loaf of wheat bread.

"This food sucks," Serafina said.

"Well, since you'll be working at that restaurant," Mom said, "you can learn how to do better."

"I need black pants and a white top," said Serafina.

"You've got black pants."

"They're a wreck."

Mom continued to eat. She seemed to be looking somewhere else, maybe to the future, where he and Serafina were grown-up and on their own. Marcus felt a heavy sadness. He swallowed hard, wishing the time was right, but it never was. Might as well say it.

"Thursday night," he began nervously, "we're finishing the paper drive at school."

His mother looked up, blinking as if she'd been almost asleep. "So?"

"We're all supposed to be at school in the afternoon, helping."

"You're still grounded, Marcus."

"But, Mom! It's a school project. It's not for fun—it's for a cause. We're raising money to redeem slaves. Don't you ever listen to me?"

"I'm listening, Marcus. You are grounded for the next month—home right after school, no exceptions. If there's one thing I've learned, it's that I won't let you kids con me anymore. I am going to know where you are and who you're with for as long as you're living under this roof. And if you disobey me, there will be consequences."

Marcus glanced at Serafina. She was looking down at her plate.

"How am I supposed to collect papers?"

"I don't know, Marcus. This conversation is over."

Marcus started on his own floor, ringing doorbells, explaining about the paper drive.

"I'll be glad to get rid of this junk," said the woman next door. She asked him in, fussing about her cat. "I just got back from work," she explained, "and Mister's been alone all day." She laughed. "I call him Mister because there's no man around—except for him."

Marcus smiled politely and waited. The woman gathered enough papers and magazines for four bundles. She was a real pack rat, Marcus figured, because next she asked whether he needed string and when he said yes, she rummaged around and found two good-sized bags full of string, cord, and rope all wound into little balls.

"Do you know where else I could get papers?" he asked.

"Across the hall. That Mr. Resnick has papers in his storeroom down in the basement. Tons of 'em."

"Will he give them to me?"

"Not to you, but to those people you told me about in Africa, the ones who need help so badly. Resnick's gruff on the outside, but he's really a pushover." She smiled, and Marcus wondered whether the two of them were friends.

"Why does he keep all those papers?"

"He's a pack rat, I guess."

All day and into the early evening, Marcus went door to door, gathering up newspapers, bringing them back to his apartment, stacking them in the living room.

When Serafina came home, she stared and pointed to her head. "Are you nuts? What do you think Mom's going to say when she sees all this? You'll get creamed."

"It's for the paper drive, for the—"

"I know, I know," Serafina said, making a face. "To free the slaves. Marcus, hasn't it ever occurred to you that you can't fix the whole world?"

"You're right," he said. "But I guess I can fix a little piece of it."

Serafina grinned and shook her head. "You're really something, you know?"

Marcus stared at his sister. She looked different—no makeup except lipstick, and her hair was tied back. She wore a plain white shirt and her old black slacks, patched on the side. Her earrings made her still look like Serafina, bright and pretty, but less flashy than before, cleaner.

"What's it like at the coffee shop?" he asked.

"It's okay." Serafina shrugged. "Today I got a three-dollar tip, just for pie à la mode and coffee."

"Do you get to keep the tips?"

"I share with the busboys. All the waitresses do."

"Do you like the other waitresses?"

"They're okay." Serafina pulled the band from her hair and shook her head. Her hair looked soft.

"You look nice," he said.

"Trying to butter me up, Marcus?"

"What can I do about all these papers?" Marcus asked.

"How should I know? It's your problem." She looked away, then turned back. "Well, I guess you could ask the maintenance guy if you could keep them in the breezeway or something. When's the paper drive?"

"Thursday. I've got five more days to go collecting."

Serafina made a face, like blowing out smoke. "Man, in five days, if you keep this up, you'll have enough to fill a bus."

Marcus laughed.

"Or a railroad car," Serafina said, laughing with him.

"Or a plane!" they said together.

"That maintenance guy's a grouch, and he hates me."

"He doesn't, either." Serafina gave him a long look. "Okay," she said. "Let's go ask him together."

Serafina talked the maintenance man into letting them stack the papers in the shed where tools and cleaning supplies were kept. Marcus carried bundles of paper until his hands were black from newsprint and his back and shoulders ached.

After five afternoons and evenings of collecting, the shed was nearly full.

The maintenance man caught Marcus bringing in another bundle and shouted, "Stop! You've got to leave space for me to get in and out. What in tarnation are you doing, anyhow?"

Marcus explained the paper drive. "We're raising money to free slaves in Sudan—kids like us. They're captured and taken away from their families and forced to work. They're mistreated, beaten—"

"Whoa," said the man. He scratched his head. "I think I read about this. The article said you kids mean well, but you're not solving the root of the problem."

Marcus stared at the man. He wished he knew the right words now; he thought of the photograph of Mother Teresa on the wall at school: DO SMALL THINGS WITH GREAT LOVE.

"Well, we're just doing what we can," Marcus said. "If it was your mom or your kid, wouldn't you want to get them free?"

"Yeah, I guess so," said the man. "But the article said you're encouraging those soldiers to take more slaves. It said if they get paid for giving 'em back, they'll just keep on taking more. It said you're creating a market in human beings!"

"No!" Marcus exclaimed. "The leaders in southern Sudan don't think so." He squared his shoulders and looked the man in the eye.

"What leaders?" The man squinted and leaned closer to Marcus, listening.

"The tribal leaders. They're the ones who arrange with the traders to get the people back. There's a man who brings money to free the slaves—fifty dollars each, no more. The price hasn't gone up in two years. That proves the article is wrong. People like to make trouble," Marcus went on heatedly. "Controversy sells papers, that's all there is to it."

"Well, I sure got more of a lesson than I bargained for," said the man, with a grin. "How do you know all this stuff?"

"My teacher, Miss Hazel, tells us the truth," said Marcus. His heart was racing. He had never talked to a grown-up person this way, had never used such words or felt so completely sure of himself.

"Well, okay," said the maintenance man. He held out his hand. "My name is Patrick." His handclasp was firm and friendly.

"Hi, Patrick," said Marcus. "Thanks a lot. I'll tell my class about your help. We're keeping a list of the people who help us."

"Mighty obliged," said Patrick. "You be sure and lock up when you're done."

"Yes, sir!"

The Escape
Adot's Story
NORTHERN SUDAN

WELL, SOMETIMES THE CALL of nature is a wonder, indeed. You may laugh at this tale; I like to hear laughter.

I am Adot, from the village of G——; yes, Adot Thiop.

How did I escape? I will tell you, but you must not laugh. I will tell you how it was. You know already how they came riding into our cattle camp, with their minds on murder and on prizes. Such prizes! They took my calf, you know, butchered him on the road that very night. I do not speak of it. Too terrible. Me, they tied tight to the horse, and I had to run. I fell once and was dragged. Dragged on the ground over stones. Here, see on my leg; it is from the stones rubbing so, and no water to clean the wound, no medicine. So it remains this color, always.

Well, everyone has a scar. Some show more, some less.

143

You ask about my escape? Well, I am telling you! They took me north, not on the train, no, but running alongside the horse, and I tell you that horse could run. I felt its sweat dropping upon my body. Sweat of a horse is thick and slimy, let me tell you, but I did not blame the horse for this. I blamed the soldiers.

Listen, it is a fact that they were so very young, no older than I. If they had not had rifles—if they had not had so many rifles—I would have wrestled them and won. I know I would have felled them. It took three to tie me. Yes, I say it proudly. They beat me that night, with sticks, only for their pleasure.

What kind of man takes pleasure in beating another? Wild men, animal men, that is the kind. They want to drink blood. Do I know why? I myself prefer milk. I am not a woman, to sit quietly and play with children, no; I love sport and wrestling and running, leaping, hunting. But this sport of man hunting man and children—no, it is not right.

So I thought maybe they are a different creature altogether, not really human. Maybe they are demons. I heard them talk of things . . . such things as you could not imagine. They spoke about women and conquest and power, and in the same breath they dared to speak of God. A holy mission, they called it, a holy war. And I cried out, "What holiness is there in this?" They heard my sounds but did not understand my words, but from my face they must have known my meaning. That was when they beat me with their sticks. I endured it well. They had no power over me. It was only their guns that held me.

Well, they feasted that night. I do not say on what they feasted, but they ate the meat and sucked the bones and boiled the hide and hoof. It is very bad for men to stuff themselves that way. Have you ever seen a fat Dinka? No, not one. Long and thin like reeds, they can bend because they eat little and modestly.

Well, these soldiers ate like animals. They ate until they groaned and stretched and made noises like no gentleman would do. And then one said, "I must go," and another grasped him by the shoulder and told his fellow, "I also am too full." So they went to the bushes, and I could peer at them to watch.

They had taken the rope and tied me to a branch. While they ate, all the while they ate, I had worked on that rope with my fingers—see, my fingers are strong and nimble from wrestling and because I do not eat too much. Eating too much makes the fingers fat. See, I worked on that rope, and it opened for me like a door, but they did not know it.

So they went to the bushes. And such a grunting and straining as came from that place!

I pulled. The rope fell away. I crept away. Dinka can creep, I tell you, without a sound. No clothes had I to make noise, no bracelets; they had stolen all. So, naked and black and sleek, I crept away into the trees, behind rocks, slowly, slowly, for still the grunting and the moaning and stink came my way, and I knew they were occupied, yes, well occupied for some time. I ran.

A Dinka can run, let me tell you, like a fox. In and out, down, around, far I ran. All night I ran, confused, and half the next day. And then I came to the market, where trading was going on, selling and buying, cursing and shouting, like music, let me tell you, music in my ears.

I saw this man, a trader in white, his eyes watching over me, and I went to him, and we stood together in the shade. "Are you free?" he asked.

"Now I am free," I said.

"Where are you going?" he asked.

"Home, if God wills."

"How can you get there safely? Do you know the way? What is the village where you live?"

I told him the village. He said, "I am going near there, bringing people to freedom. A man comes to redeem them with money."

"I do not need redemption," I told this trader, "but I will go with you to find the way. Is it well with you that I go?"

"Yes, you can look out for some of the weak ones. The children. You can help, for I see that you are strong and clever, having escaped."

So I tell the trader, "Yes, we are brothers traveling together. But it is not that I am so very strong or clever to manage escape. It is the fault of the soldiers themselves, who are gluttons, eating like animals." So you see, this is what happens when men do not follow the Dinka way of moderation. They lose.

Small Things
Marcus's Story
WESTERN UNITED STATES

Serafina brought hamburgers home from the restaurant, and french fries in waxed paper bags, and little tubes of mustard and ketchup.

"Where's Mom?" she asked Marcus.

"Working late again, I guess," he said.

"Oh, great. Just when I bring in dinner."

"We can save it for her."

"I wanted her to have it while it was warm," said Serafina. "Well, who cares?"

"I do. This is great." He took a big bite of the burger, chewing fast.

"Why are you so jumpy?"

"Colin and his dad are coming at seven to pick up my newspapers," he said. "I hope they get here before Mom does."

"Oh yeah. Mom might give them a bad time," said Serafina.

"Why does she always do that?"

The buzzer rang. Marcus leaped up. He called out to Colin, who was taking the stairs two at a time. "Hey! Wait, I'll meet you downstairs. The papers are out in the shed in the breezeway."

But Colin was already on the landing, followed by his dad, and suddenly everything was in commotion, for Mom was standing behind them, looking surprised and anxious, asking, "What's going on here, Marcus? Where are you going?"

Colin's dad smiled and held out his hand, saying, "I'm Colin's dad, Fred Kester. We've come to pick up the newspapers for the paper drive at school."

And then everybody was talking at once. Mom was saying, "Yes, of course," but Marcus could tell she had forgotten all about it. She looked baffled, then embarrassed.

"Won't you come in?" she finally asked, pushing the door open. Marcus could see her checking out the room. He had put away his pillow and blanket; Serafina had taken the bags and leftover fries off the table. The place looked decent. He was relieved.

"Come in," Mom repeated. "Please, have a seat. I just got home from work. How about a Coke, Mr. Kester?"

"Sounds great. I haven't had dinner yet. Colin was pushing me out the door to get here!"

Mom served Cokes to everyone, using the tall blue glasses she'd bought at the Pottery Palace. She shook a bag of pretzels into a colorful basket, smiling, saying, "It isn't exactly dinner, but this might take the edge off."

"We'd better get over to the school," Colin said nervously. "Miss Hazel says we have to be finished by nine."

"Take it easy, son," said Colin's dad. "Just give me two minutes to finish this drink." He leaned toward Mom. "These kids are really great, aren't they? I wish there were a thousand Miss Hazels in the district. She really makes them work, plus she focuses on the important things."

"Yes," said Mom faintly, "Marcus seems to like her a lot."

"I wanted to ask you something," said Mr. Kester. "Colin tells me that Marcus has been trying to sell that old Ted Williams baseball card he found at the mall. Apparently that man at the hobby store didn't give him a fair offer."

Marcus felt a flush spreading over his face as his mother stared at him in wonderment. "What kind of a card would that be?" she asked in a strained tone.

Now Mr. Kester looked uncomfortable. "Didn't Marcus tell you about it?"

Serafina said, "Isn't a card like that worth a lot of money?"

"You bet it is," said Mr. Kester. "According to my catalog that card could bring up to three hundred dollars."

"Three hundred?" Marcus's mom looked from one to the other. Her eyes fastened on Marcus. Her expression reproached him more than words could. Her eyes signaled something; later they would talk about this.

"Well, I thought I'd like to make a bid on that card," said Colin's father. "We're trying to build our collection. Of course,

I'd rather not pay top dollar, but I would want to be perfectly fair. Colin tells me the man at the store offered Marcus only fifty dollars."

"Marcus has been pretty busy," said his mom, gazing at him. "I hope he didn't take fifty dollars for something worth more than five times that much."

"I didn't," Marcus said quickly.

"Maybe the two of you would discuss what you think is a fair price," said Mr. Kester, putting down his empty glass. "We could talk about it another time. Right now, we'd better get those newspapers to school before Colin jumps out the window."

They all laughed and headed down the stairs to the shed. Patrick had kept it unlocked for Marcus, and now, as Marcus pushed open the door and turned on the light, everyone seemed to explode with amazement.

"Wow! Did you do all this, Marcus?"

"It's impossible—how could you?"

"You've got more papers here than half the class!" Colin exclaimed.

"Okay, let's get these loaded up," said Mr. Kester. He sized up the papers and shook his head. "I don't think all this will fit into my trunk."

"I can take a load in my car," said Mom. "Ask Serafina to come and help load up," she told Marcus. She turned to Colin. "We don't want to be late, do we?"

It was sort of like a dream; better than a dream, Marcus thought—being the best, having the most, hearing praise from kids and parents and Miss Hazel. By the time all his papers were unloaded, it was clear that he had collected nearly five times as much as anyone else.

"And you did it all alone," said Miss Hazel. "And you never told anyone."

While Marcus and the others were loading the newspapers onto a large truck to be taken away, Miss Hazel and his mother stood off to one side, talking. Once in a while Marcus glanced up at them, wishing he could hear. They both looked so serious. One time, his mom was nodding and laughing, and he felt a surge of joy.

It was after ten when they got home, because many of the parents stayed for an impromptu meeting, talking about the slave issue and what they could do, saying how proud they were of their children. Seeing his mom with the other parents, Marcus had a different view. She looked younger than most mothers, pale and delicate. Her sweater was faded, her shoes a little shabby. But when she looked his way and gave him a big smile, Marcus smiled back, then he gave Colin a poke just because he was so happy he didn't know what else to do.

At home, Marcus's mother beckoned to him to sit down beside her on the couch. He edged away, feeling embarrassed. She said, "Do you want to sell your baseball card to Mr. Kester?"

Marcus was surprised. "Aren't you going to ask me about it? How I found it? Why I didn't tell you?"

His mother turned to him, her expression intent—a little sad but resigned. "I suppose you didn't tell me because you felt I wouldn't really listen." She sighed. "Maybe you didn't trust me."

"I trust you, Mom!"

She held up her hand. "You didn't ask me to take you to the mall. You didn't ask me to come with you to sell the card."

"I know. I'm sorry."

"Maybe you just wanted to prove your independence," she said.

Marcus said nothing. Maybe that was it; maybe something less noble.

"So, do you want to sell it to Colin's dad?"

"I guess so. Sure."

"What do you think is a fair price?"

"I don't know. What do you think?"

His mom frowned, contemplating. "Less than three hundred dollars, I guess, because that's the dealer's price. More than fifty."

"Two hundred," said Marcus. "I think that's fair."

"All right. You can tell Colin tomorrow. What are you going to do with the money?"

"I thought I'd buy a bike," Marcus whispered.

"That sounds like a good idea. What about rules? Would you wear a helmet? Would you always tell me before you go out?"

"I'd follow the rules," Marcus said softly. "But I feel rotten all the same."

His mother leaned toward him. For once she didn't look tired. "Why?"

"Because Serafina needs money for black pants, and you

could use the money for your old clunker, like you're always saying."

"Look, Marcus, that money is yours, fair and square. Since you found the card at the mall, we'd never locate the true owner. Someone just dropped it. Bad luck for them, good luck for you. As for Serafina, she can earn money from her job to buy herself the pants. I'm working and saving for a new car. You deserve a bike. You don't have to take care of everyone else. Charity is for those who really can't help themselves."

He nodded. "That's what Miss Hazel says."

"Miss Hazel," said his mother, "is a gem. One in a million. You are one heck of a lucky kid."

Marcus had not planned to do it. Everything came together the following week, when the congressman came into their classroom. He was neither tall nor heavyset, but somehow he seemed larger than life. Maybe it came from a certain glow in his eyes, a friendliness in his smile, the firmness of his handshake. He shook hands with Miss Hazel first, then with Marcus and the other children.

"I have had the privilege," he said, standing in front of the class, "of visiting Sudan, last month. What I saw with my own eyes is exactly what you boys and girls have been telling the world through your letters and your personal commitment—that slavery does exist, that we must take action, that our action will make a difference. It is already starting to make a difference. I spoke to some of the Dinka leaders. They asked me, 'Who are these children in America who care about us?'"

Marcus felt a huge, overpowering sense of gladness, a warmth spreading throughout his entire body. He glanced at the bulletin board with its many pictures, then at the photograph of Mother Teresa. And he knew in that moment what the caption meant. What is a small thing to one person can be a great thing to another. It was almost as if he wasn't really making a decision, as if it had been his intention all along.

He looked around the room at his friends. All of them were turned to the congressman, listening intently, smiling, feeling a bond.

"I am proud to present you with a gift," said the congressman, turning to Miss Hazel. "I am giving you this American flag, which has flown over the White House. It is a symbol of freedom. I know you will think of a good place to display it."

"Thank you so much, Congressman," said Miss Hazel. She dabbed at her eyes with her handkerchief. All the kids were beaming. "I know exactly how we will display this flag," she said. "We will hang it in the auditorium. But first we will take a trip up to the mountains and hold it out, so that we'll all remember this day."

"When are we going?" asked Marcus.

"As soon as we can get transportation," said Miss Hazel. "This week, if possible."

It took several days to arrange for cars and permission slips. During that time, Colin and his parents, and Marcus and his mother all got together once again. Mr. Kester added the Ted Williams card to his collection, and he gave Marcus two beautiful one-hundred-dollar bills. Marcus held them in his hand. He had never seen such bills before, and it would be a long, long time until he did again.

All night he could hardly sleep for his excitement.

In his dreams people were dancing, clasping hands, singing. All kinds of people came together on a mountaintop, children and grown-ups, all singing the same song.

In the morning, when he was leaving for school, Marcus's mom stopped him.

"How about a kiss good-bye?"

He grinned. "Oh, Mom." She kissed him lightly and straightened his collar.

"Are you sure you want to do this?" she asked.

"Yes. I'm sure."

"Okay," she said. "You better go then. Take care."

"I will."

He went off to school, walking fast, not running. The money was secure in his pocket, but he wasn't taking any chances. People depended on this money. Four people were going to be free. Because of him.

Mercy
The Man's Story
DINKALAND, SOUTHERN SUDAN

MERCY, MERCY—NO WORDS can explain or take the place of mercy. Listen, my children, and then we will go to the fields to pick the sweet sugarcane.

It is a day like many others, yet it is like no other day ever lived.

Sunlight glares onto asphalt. In the fields, sunlight shimmers above raw earth, a floating mirage. Dryness crackles underfoot, chafes the skin, cracks the lips.

The people walk. Their collective steps form a slow, shuffling serenade. They do not speak; their energy is given only to walking. Some have been walking for three days. Along the way, they are joined by others, who slip quickly into the line, adding their tuneless song to the rest.

It is a song of hope, sung only in the heart. They have been moved too many times already; they have been too long without choices. And now, still, they move in only one direction and at a regulated pace. Where are they going? They have been told little. Words whispered in the night, the flash of a beacon, commands. "Come! Hurry! Do not make a sound."

"But where are we going? Is it safe? Is it possible?"

"We are setting you free."

"Free? You mean *now*? Tonight?"

"You must walk, trust me! We will walk to freedom."

And so, as they walk, they begin to murmur, sharing their stories, each one a tale of horror and misery, each a small miracle of redemption. That they are alive at all is a wonder. They look at each other in amazement. And they walk on.

There is water for some, warm and rusty, carried in an old can or, with luck, a plastic bottle salvaged from some relief caravan bringing oil or flour or corn. There is no food now. Some eat leaves that they swiftly rip from shrubs as they go. Better not to eat them, the older ones advise; it is even harder to walk with cramps in the belly and needing to run to the bushes for relief.

"But where are we going? When we arrive, where will we be? Will anyone come to meet us? Who knows we are coming? Who knows our names?"

"The Man. The Man knows."

"How does he know?"

"The Man has secret ways. He finds us and sends for us."

"What sort of man is it that would care about us?"

"They say he is a white man."

"White man? Since when does white man come to save those who are black?"

"The Man does not think of color."

"Such a one does not live, I think, without color in his mind."

"The Man does not think of color. He thinks of souls."

"Ah, he is a minister, then, or a priest?"

"No. He is only a man."

"It costs money, plenty, to free people. It is the price of two goats or even a cow. Who has so much money to spare? What stranger would bring money for people like us? We cannot pay him back!"

"The Man brings money; he gathers it up like figs from a tree. They say, so holy is the Man that when he walks by, the fruits turn into coins of gold and silver, jingling on the branches like little bells. He plucks them off and puts them into a sack. So holy is he that the birds and the serpents in the trees stop to watch. It is a great miracle."

"No, no, it is not so. The truth is this: The Man speaks with a silver tongue, pleading for money for us. Great leaders bow to him and reach into their vaults and bring him money in sacks. They bring much gold, these great ones, who otherwise never dip into their treasuries without wanting something in return. That is the miracle."

"No, no, it is not so. No person can carry that much money! The Man brings but a little, and as he sets it down for the trader, the money grows ever more, like the loaves and fishes we hear about in church. It increases by itself; that is the miracle."

They ponder the Man. *Where is he from? How was he shaped, and by what circumstances has he become like a saint while he yet lives? Who knows the story?*

WELL, HERE IS THE STORY: The Man was born far away in Australia, a native aborigine, in the outback. As a small child he lived well with his people, and he learned many skills. He was a champion with the spear, both for fishing and hunting. He was a great wrestler, winning matches with boys much older and stronger than he. Even as a young boy, the Man had the nature of one who wins by concentration and power of the mind. Thus, his early training made him fit for the rigors of a journey and to stand firm against attack.

Once, they say, when he was still a boy, he was attacked by a pack of wolves. You will see that after some many miles of walking, the Man limps a little. It is from the attack, where the leader wolf caught him by the right ankle and held on fiercely. The Man caught the wolf around the throat and wrestled him to the ground. It was a great victory, celebrated among the Man's people in song and dance.

Now he comes to us, bringing his strength and seeking adventure. For our land is one of the few where adventure and challenge still abound. It is a land of wild creatures, alligator and hippopotamus. Once, after the heavy rains, the Man came to Sudan to see us. Hippopotamus had crept out from the river, following the rain. Hippopotamus came into our camp, even to the hut of our uncle, threatening the crops and the children. The Man ran out and stood straight in front of that hippopotamus. He raised his arms and commanded it: "Go back to the river, I command you! Leave my people in peace!" And the beast did stare at him for a long moment, and then it abruptly turned away and was never seen on land again.

You see, the Man has a special connection with the animals. Their instinct tells them of his goodness. It is always so with a saint. Animals and children recognize him at once. When you see the Man, you will feel it, too.

WELL, HERE IS THE STORY: The Man was born in a distant land, a country in South America. Argentina, it is called, and songs are sung about it, a beautiful land with much cattle. His people had lived there for generations. They lived on the land, farmers, tilling and toiling and making cheese. They lived in comfort with plenty to eat until the time came when neighbors began to oppress them. It was a matter of differences and greed over land and water.

Grazing rights and water rights, always in dispute, flare up sometimes, and neighbors who were friends become enemies overnight. And the regime rekindled old rivalries, urging one group to make war against another. The regime, you see, wanted to conquer and subdue the people. There was intrigue aplenty and gathering of weapons—knives, guns, fire.

In the night, when the Man was a small boy, suddenly the barn was on fire, cattle bellowing, one chicken running with all its feathers in flames. The boy and his family—mother, father, sisters, and old grandparents—ran out to find buckets and bottles and cups to bring water. But wind from the south blew up, and also from the east, and wind meeting wind caused the fire to fly across the field to the house. The fire roared inside. Beams and walls and roof soon ignited with flames hot and red that took down the house so fast, nothing could be saved. Flames spread to their storehouses. Gone was the cheese, the grain and corn, the fruits saved in the cellar, all gone.

Now destitute, the small boy and his family wandered from place to place, always seeking shelter, but none would take them in. They came to a camp, a place where the dispossessed had been told to find food. But there they were forced to hear of things they found abominations—lies. They were forced to repeat and practice these things in exchange for food, to take a faith that they did not know or believe. And so the Man grew up knowing what it is to be forced into a lie, the cutting of the soul into two parts—one part love, the other part guilt for betraying that love.

The Man knows our pain and our guilt. He knows how we have been forced to eat food we do not know, say words we do not mean, answer to names we do not own, and give our bodies to people whose ways are foreign and evil to us. Because he knows this, the Man comes to redeem us. It is the debt he pays for his own redemption, for he was freed one day from this bondage, and now he in turn frees us.

WELL, HERE IS THE STORY: The Man was living in peace in the heart of Europe, as a very small child. But a great war came, and many people were rounded up by soldiers with guns. These people were put into trains. The sides were boarded up.

They were packed in like cattle bound for the slaughterhouse, like chickens in crates, all staring. They were sent to distant places, forced to labor, starved, and beaten. Many, many were killed.

The Man had a father and a mother who saw what was happening to their neighbors. They said all roads lead to the same maker, isn't it so? They said that if we do not save them, if we do not hear their cries, we become conspirators, too; we become providers of evil.

The father of the Man went out every day onto the road. He opened his eyes and his ears. When he saw a person frightened and fleeing, he went to this person and spoke soft words to let the trust show, and he took this person home. His father had built a secret cellar under the floor. There he took the poor hunted ones and hid them safe. He provided a bed and food and water, even books and a candle. For a person must also fill his mind with learning, not just sit in dismal silence and darkness.

For four years this was the case; the secret room was a chapel, a sanctuary in the midst of ruin. Into that secret place came parents with small children. Sometimes it was one old person alone in the world. Sometimes it was an infant who had to be nourished and taught not to cry. All in all, forty-seven people, young and old, well and sick, lived in that small room and were later sent in secret to safety.

The Man, who was still a small boy, saw all this. He learned everything about human beings. He saw his mother tending their wounds and washing their clothes, cooking their food, speaking encouragement. He saw his father face danger every day. He saw tears. He also saw the light of gratitude shining in people's eyes. He learned what happiness was. The Man now walks in the steps of his father, and the father looks down from heaven and knows that his own head had been lifted up with pride by the works of his son.

These are the stories: Everyone believes he has the true story of the Man.

The people walk on, keeping to the sides of the road, creeping into the thick cover of bushes and trees. They walk in the night, when the moon glows to give them a path. They walk early in the morning to spare themselves the full heat of midday, but still the heat clothes them like a robe, like a blanket. *When will we see the Man?* They are curious, but not eager. They have not the strength for eagerness, only the exhausted whisper, When?

I will tell you about the Man who is coming now.

He brings an old case packed with clothes, a thin blanket, and some medicine against fevers. He has left his home very early in the morning. He has kissed his wife, who no longer weeps but gazes at him in a deep quietness. She will not beg him not to go. She cannot ask this of him. She prays silently for his safe return, for it is a dangerous journey.

His sons stand at the window and wave their good-byes. The older one wishes his father were home to see his ball game. He feels lonely when the fathers of the other boys shout and laugh and praise their sons for a fine game. The seat beside his mother is empty. His father is far away, in Africa. When people ask him, Where is your dad? he shakes his head and says briefly, "At work." The son feels proud that he is trusted with the truth. His father is going to free some people in Africa.

The little one sucks his thumb. He does not understand why Father has to leave, or why when he returns he is different. The child is too young to know that a man going on such a mission is changed by it, every time.

The man travels for many hours. He tries to sleep. The drone of the airplane, and its jolts, keep him awake. Also the thought of his wife alone with the children, the thought of what could happen to them if he does not return—all these keep sleep away.

At last he arrives in the large city, and he is met there by the bishop and his assistant, and by a few other men. He no longer feels strange with his white face and his city clothes. He sees himself mirrored in *their* faces, and they are smiling, with shining eyes and outstretched hands. In a way, he is home.

The Man sleeps briefly on a cot in a room. Soon it is time to go to the airport, not the great airport where he arrived but a small place where old planes are kept and flown by pilots who have known war and other disasters. Again and again the Man looks at his watch. The plane must touch down before nightfall, for there are no landing lights. There is no airport, only a road cleared of brush and debris. If the bombers come, he and the others will rush to hide under the trees.

The Man would like to bring food and medicine and clothing. But the small airplane is cramped, and besides, he must walk many hours to come to the meeting place, and he cannot carry very much. The Man is not muscular or large;

he is an ordinary man of ordinary size. His eyes are gray, his hair, light brown. His hands do not move in the manner of an orator; he speaks softly.

At last the plane comes, then takes off, rumbling. The flight is full of vibration. Not only the aircraft but thoughts vibrate. The Man feels anger at the soldiers and the regime, at the cause that makes them hunt these people down. The Man yearns to liberate them. He has seen their faces before. He has shaken their hands, touched a shoulder; he has been there, and he knows. He must see them once more. To liberate is a sweet thing, a heady thing, more potent than wine.

Critics complain. Some say he has, with his money, caused more slaves to be taken. It is not true, but people love an argument. Some say it is unwise to interfere. After all, this country has its own government and its own laws. The Man says that laws that oppress people are wrong. Some say that he opposes Islam. He will say he only opposes those who pervert Islam. Some say he is too simple. The Man says that justice is simple: Do right.

He arrives. It is nearly dark. He runs from the plane, hearing rumbling overhead. If they shoot him down, who will set the slaves free? He knows they are walking to meet him, walking for days in the hot sun. His friends run to greet him. Some are dressed in soldier's garb, fighting for freedom from the regime. Some are chiefs, surrounded by the elders of their villages. Their smiles are wide, their hands clasping his arms. The people make songs about the Man. The people sing and clap their hands when he appears. The Man only smiles. His face reddens. He does not wish to be praised.

The chiefs walk beside him now, together setting their faces to the north. As they walk, the chiefs explain how each person was found. The traders are the link. They have always been a link between tribes, bringing offers of peace, making treaties for trade and water rights. One hand washes the other, as the saying goes. You may graze on my land; I will sell hides and sugarcane at your market. You may use water from my well; in return, you will find my people who are captured. Of course, there is a price—to free captives is risky. One must be paid for the risk.

The Man worries. What if the trader was caught? What if the bombers come and drop death on the assembled crowd? What if the walk was too hard and some have died along the way? It happens.

The Man walks on. Blisters form on his feet. The water in his bottle is warm, and there is never enough to last. The trek is long. Was it so long the last time? Or does he grow impatient?

He sees nothing on the horizon, but the donkey walking beside his guide seems to hearken. Its ears twitch forward, its nostrils flare.

Now the Man sees a cloud of dust at a great distance. It spreads and rises. Closer, closer. The Man hears the shuffling of feet, an occasional cough, and then, voices.

Into the clearing they come, the long line of black bodies bringing a catch to the Man's throat, a stinging to his eyes. His hands move to his mouth. He waits. He squints. The tall man clad in traditional white *gallabiya* has concealed his face with the edges of his head cloth. Only his eyes look out. They dart and flicker. He is afraid, too.

The Man takes a step forward. He speaks. "Karim, is it you?"

"Yes, my friend. It is I."

"Peace, peace to you, my friend. And are you well?" The Man speaks the courtesies of Islam.

"*Sallam Alleikum,* my friend. Is it well with you, too?"

"All is well. And the people?"

"None died on the way, praise Allah."

"Praise God."

"We have the names, certificates for each."

"I have the money."

"We will trade."

"Let us do so now."

All the people move into the shade of a huge mahogany tree. Its branches seem to widen as they cluster under it, expanding to shield their bodies.

The Man sits down on a rock. He has brought a satchel. He opens it now. The zipper makes a sound. Nobody moves. The satchel falls open.

And now the barter begins.

Time seems to stretch and strain. The trade goes on. The money moves from hand to hand, from the Man's satchel to the trader's sack. The Man grows weary, but he does not move from his place on the rock.

And then it is over. Each freedom has been bought. The Man moves into the circle of people standing in the shade of the great mahogany tree. He stands before them, hands at his sides.

They wait: Dabora Achol Amou; Kwol, son of Biong; and all the others. They have seen the money change hands. Have they been sold again to a new master? Is this only a trick?

The Man speaks. "You are free," he says. "By the grace of God and with the help of many people whose names you will never know, you are free."

A name is called. "Dabora Achol Amou."

She steps out from the shelter of branches. Confusion fills her eyes, and dread. Who is this coming for her? A new master perhaps? Was it all a trick only to rob her once again of herself?

No. She strains to see; the dust has clouded her eyes. It is the Old One and—and a lovely girl; yes, a girl nearly grown to womanhood. And in the next moment, as the girl runs to her, mouth wide with love and with laughter, she knows. "Amou! Daughter!"

Who can speak of reunion and do justice to the truth of it? Feelings of freedom cannot be described. All around, the same scene is repeated—cries and murmurs and silences that speak more than words. "Brother!" "Father!" "Mother!" "Child!"

Words, handclasps, recognition—"Are you Kwol from the village of B——, and were you captured as a young boy?"

"Yes! Yes! And my father, Biong, does he still live?"

"He lives, I assure you. Come, we go to him."

All around, the stories are told, new children are seen for the first time, husbands greet wives, sisters embrace after long emptiness.

The Man picks up his satchel. He turns to the chief. "Time to go," he says. "Thank you."

The chief and his assistants bring the Man back to the border, to the plane that takes him out of the country, then home.

By nightfall the Man is well on his way, but the people newly freed do not travel yet. No, there is too much to say; there are too many stories to tell and smiles to give and songs to sing. And as night deepens, their long agony lifts away like a mist. They begin to sway. They begin to dance. Through the night they sing and dance. And they tell stories.

They tell stories about the Man and who has sent him, what manner of childhood shaped him, what hardships prepared him for this task.

And I will tell you the truth: He is a man of mercy. That is all there is to know.

Author's Note
The History of Sudan

Sudan, a large country in northeast Africa, is a land in conflict. Differences in race, religion, and ideas about leadership have caused sharp divisions between the Arab people of the north and the native Dinka and Nuba people of the south. The people of Sudan hold various religious beliefs: Some are devout Muslims, some have adopted Christianity, others have maintained their native faith based on the worship of one God.

The Sudanese people have been engaged in sporadic civil war since they gained independence from British rule in 1956. Since then, various governments have held power, trying to unify the country, with only occasional periods of peace. In 1989 the emergence of a new government widened the rift between north and south. Many southern groups wished to form their own government and secede, while the northern rulers demanded conformity to their beliefs and system of government.

Famine, both natural and man-made, has added to the suffering in southern Sudan. In this civil war, more than 1.9 million people in southern and central Sudan have died, and more than 4 million southern Sudanese have been forced to flee their homes. The land has been devastated, its people scattered, crops and houses destroyed.

One terrifying weapon of war has been the capture and enslavement of thousands of people, mostly women and children, by northern armies in their raids upon southern villages. Reports of chattel slavery have been investigated and verified by international human rights organizations and by U.S. government representatives and by various news agencies.

Those involved in this bitter conflict recognize that while war is the primary cause of this human catastrophe, slavery is its most horrifying consequence. Can the nations and the peoples of the world work together to find a solution to both evils?

Afterword

by Barbara Vogel
THE FOUNDER, WITH HER
FIFTH-GRADE STUDENTS, OF S.T.O.P.

What you have just read is at once terrible and inspirational. The depiction of slavery in *Dream Freedom* is not history, nor is it fiction—it is reality for tens of thousands of men, women, and children at the very moment you read this. I know because I visited Sudan in October of 1999 to observe a remarkable emancipation mission that freed 4,300 slaves. There I heard the shocking stories and saw the deep pain in children's eyes—but I also witnessed the unparalleled joy of freedom.

Three years ago, it was that vision of freedom that inspired my fifth-grade students to take a stand against modern-day slavery in Sudan. Our class happened upon this atrocity while reading a short newspaper article, but the story changed our lives. Realizing that adults were not doing enough to protect African children from slave raids, my students resolved to work for a better future for children everywhere, and to launch the S.T.O.P. (Slavery That Oppresses People) abolitionist campaign.

Today that campaign has been adopted as a model for hundreds of schools around the world where students learn about contemporary slavery, educate their communities, and take action. There are now thousands of students acting as responsible human beings and responding to the worst form of human rights abuse. Indeed, this is the largest abolitionist movement since the United States Civil War.

These students do not pity their besieged and decimated brothers and sisters; rather, they respect them. By standing up for the rights of people whom adult leaders had abandoned, students have issued a call to action: "Everybody has a responsibility to make the world a better place." In doing so, these children embody the best of the American commitment to liberty and justice for all, and they help our country reclaim its abolitionist heritage.

These student abolitionists have a special message for you: "Join us." The fight to end modern-day slavery is really about you—about how you will use your freedom. We know you will reach out to help free those who remain in bondage. And then you can say, in the words of abolitionist Harriet Tubman: "I have heard their groans and seen their tears, and I would give every drop of blood in my veins to free them."

WHAT YOU CAN DO

1. LEARN MORE ABOUT MODERN-DAY SLAVERY

On the Web

American Anti-Slavery Group   www.anti-slavery.org
Christian Solidarity International   www.csi-int.org
U.S. Committee for Refugees   www.refugees.org

From Books

Disposable People: New Slavery in the Global Economy by
   Kevin Bales (Berkeley: University of California Press, 1999).
Silent Terror: A Journey into Contemporary African Slavery by
   Samuel Cotton (New York: Harlem Rivers Press, 1998).

2. SPREAD THE WORD

Write letters to your representatives and senators in Congress.
Inform others about what you have learned.
Invite speakers to your school, club, or town.
Join antislavery groups or start a new chapter.
Raise money to free slaves in Sudan and to provide relief.

CONTACT INFORMATION

1. American Anti-Slavery
Group
198 Tremont Street, no. 421
Boston, MA 02116
Telephone: 1-800-884-0719
2. Christian Solidarity
International
Zelglistrasse 64
P.O. Box 70
CH-8122 Binz
Zurich, Switzerland

3. S.T.O.P. Campaign
Telephone: 1-800-844-0719
4. Sudan Relief & Rescue, Inc.
P.O. Box 1877
Washington, D.C. 20013-1877
Telephone: 1-888-488-0348

Bibliography

BOOKS

Cotton, Samuel. *Silent Terror: A Journey into Contemporary African Slavery.* New York: Harlem Rivers Press, 1998.

Deng, Francis Mading. *The Cry of the Owl: A Novel.* New York: Lilian Barber Press, 1989.

———. *Dinka Cosmology.* London: Ithaca Press, 1980.

———. *Dinka Folktales: African Stories from the Sudan.* New York: Africana Publishing Company, 1974.

———. *The Dinka of Sudan.* Prospect Heights, Ill.: Waveland Press, 1984.

———. *The Man Called Deng Majok: A Biography of Power, Polygyny, and Change.* New Haven and London: Yale University Press, 1986.

———. *War of Visions: Conflict of Identities in the Sudan.* Washington, D.C.: Brookings Institution, 1995.

Gordon, Murray. *Slavery in the Arab World.* New York: New Amsterdam Books, 1989.

PAMPHLETS

American Anti-Slavery Group. *Anti-Slavery Report.* Winter 1998–99.

Meyer, Gabriel. *A Hidden Gift: War and Faith in Sudan.* Studio City, Ca.: Windhover Forum, 1999.

U.S. Committee for Refugees. *Sudan: Personal Stories of Sudan's Uprooted People.* Washington, D.C.: 1999.

U.S. House. 106th Congress. *Congressional Record.* "Congress Must Help the People of Southern Sudan," 2 March 1999.

ARTICLES

Bauer, Gary L., and Eugene F. Rivers. "U.S. Can't Neglect Sudan's Sorry State." *Boston Herald,* 6 February 1999.

Hentoff, Nat. "Anybody Care about Black Slaves?" *Village Voice,* 12 August 1998.

Jacobs, Charles. "Bought and Sold." *New York Times,* 13 July 1994.

———. "In Sudan a 12-Year-Old Girl Can Be Bought for $50." *Los Angeles Times,* 28 December 1998.

Jacobson, Linda. "Liberating Lesson." *Education Week,* 31 March 1999.

Ottaway, David B. "U.S. Eased Law to Aid Oil Firm." *Washington Post,* 23 January 1997.

Saunders, William. "Christmas in Sudan." *First Things,* May 1999.

———. "The Slaughter of the Innocents." *Catholic World Report,* May 1999.

Sink, Mindy. "Schoolchildren Set Out to Buy Freedom for Slaves." *New York Times,* 2 December 1998.

Slobodian, Linda. "Humanity for Sale." Parts 1–8. *Calgary Sun,* 1997.

U.S. Committee for Refugees. "News and Updates: Sudan." Washington, D.C., 1998.

"Where Children Live in Bondage." Parts 1–3. *Baltimore Sun,* 16–18 June 1996.

"Women and Children Saved from Slavery." *Marie Claire,* March 1999.

Woodbury, Richard. "The Children's Crusade: How Fourth and Fifth Graders in Colorado Are Buying the Freedom of Slaves in a Faraway Land." *Time,* 21 December 1998.

WEB SITES

www.anti-slavery.org
www.csi-int.org
www.refugees.org

VIDEOS

CBS Evening News. 1 February 1999. Dan Rather. "Slavery is alive and well in the Sudan, and many Americans are fighting to free those in bondage."

CBS Evening News. 2 February 1999. Dan Rather. "Barbara Vogel's students in Aurora, Colorado, raised over $70,000 to free the slaves in Sudan."

Dateline. NBC, 10 December 1996. Jane Pauley. "Spotlight on slavery."

A Hidden Gift. First Assembly, 1999. The Windhover Forum.

Slavery in Sudan. Christian Solidarity International.

S.T.O.P. Barbara Vogel's Class Antislavery Campaign.

PERSONAL INTERVIEWS

Dr. Francis Mading Deng, author and Senior Fellow at Brookings Institution, Washington, D.C.; former ambassador from Sudan.

John Eibner, abolitionist working with Christian Solidarity International, Zurich, Switzerland.

Dennis Gura, head of the Los Angeles branch of the American Anti-Slavery Group in Los Angeles.

Charles Jacobs, president of the American Anti-Slavery Group, based in Boston, with several branches, one recently formed in Los Angeles.

Professor Jok Madut Jok, African history professor, Loyola Marymount University, Los Angeles.

William Saunders, assistant to Bishop Gassis of Sudan; executive director, Sudan Relief & Rescue, Inc.; and human rights attorney, Washington, D.C.

Tom Tancredo, Colorado congressman, Washington, D.C.

Barbara Vogel, fourth- and fifth-grade teacher and founder of S.T.O.P. movement to free slaves, Denver, Colorado.